Mun.

by

B. Catling

Swan River Press
Dublin, Ireland
MMXXI

Munky
by B. Catling

Published by
Swan River Press
Dublin, Ireland
in January MMXXI

www.swanriverpress.ie
brian@swanriverpress.ie

Cover design by Meggan Kehrli
from artwork © Dave McKean

Set in Garamond by Ken Mackenzie

Published with assistance from Dublin UNESCO
City of Literature and Dublin City Libraries

Paperback Edition
ISBN 978-1-78380-745-1

Swan River Press published a limited hardback
edition of *Munky* in July 2020.

Contents

Munky

Munky

For
Shirley Collins

Waxy

Pulborough Abbey had been a site of pilgrimage for hundreds of years, its doors open to thousands of travellers: tramps and visionaries; possessed Flanners; the halt and the lame; and those seeking shelter from the weather. All had sought sanctuary inside its portals, but when the large monk arrived, the worthies of the august church talked about closing it up and barring the way against trespass.

The first three days of his occupation went unnoticed. He sat midway in a midway pew without interference or intervention. On the fourth day, a small family party, who were seeking the consolation of a toilet more than the sanctity of the house of God, asked him for directions.

"I's ain't here," he said.

"What?" said the mother after letting his words fall and bounce against her irritation.

The father, who was holding the hands of the two dancing children, joined in the inquisition.

"Well, where are they?" he asked.

His wife was about to answer when the monk said, "I's ain't here."

There hadn't been monks at the abbey since 1600. Not living ones, that is. Many parishioners had seen shadows passing through the walls, or bumped into something that wasn't there, where the cloisters had once skulked. Old Mary Vanes and her daughter Edith had seen them when they were polishing the pews in their own inimitable way, by wrapping a large waxy duster around one of the hassocks and shuffling it back and forth under their bottoms, administering the lavender balm like wormy dogs on grass.

"Who be they, Ma?"

"Pays 'em no attention and they'll do the same for you. They's just about their business as are we about ours."

The sliding Vanes turned their eyes from the hollow scar in the wall where once stood a door and concentrated on the sheen of the wood under their prodigious rhythmic rumps.

At the beginning there was little doubt about the corporality of the monk on the pew. He was large, in his late fifties, and unwashed, bearing the authentic scent of a medieval brotherhood that lived in a cold wet country in communal poverty: a virtuous odour of wood-smoke, urine, overcooked cabbage, and frozen perspiration, all saturated into his thick brown cassock and awaiting the slightest trace of warmth or friction to be released.

It was on the fourth day that the Verger Cedric Chyme informed the Canon of the peculiarity that was occurring. Chyme had not seen the unshaven ruffian who was masquerading as a monk, but others had, and word had found its way back to him, of course. Chyme took the responsibilities of his dignified office very seriously. There were times, when he was alone in the great abbey, that he felt its breath: the centuries of undefiled splendour passing through its aisles and echoing in its vaulted hammer beams. The sweeping majesty of its undecorated walls solidly stood to confirm his undaunted faith. It had stood against the corruption and greed of Papists, kings, and noblemen, held back the rising tide of the unwashed scum that surrounded it. If he could have his way he would seal it forever, only allowing scholars and those as pious as he to enter. And even they would be very few after he had weeded out the frauds and the unworthy. That should be the true role of a Verger: a keeper, protector, and holy turnkey who would vet all those who dared to demand ingress. It must have been like that in the Good Ol' Days, when they were allowed to carry arms to shoo off the peasants and beggars, and hack foreigners apart before they even spoke. Now anybody was let in. All manner of riff-raff would despoil its stillness with their uninformed curiosity: even the other workers of upkeep and divinity lacked any real understanding and knowledge of the abbey's meaning; even the pompous choirmaster; even the clergy, all of whom had agreed with the parochial council about the installation of a toilet. A PUBLIC TOILET at the far end of the inner cloister. It had been hit upon as a means of securing secular funds for a few basic improvements and placing the abbey firmly on the tourist map. A GIFT SHOP had also been planned.

Chyme's blood boiled when "visitors" came into his abbey to take shelter from the weather. Now it seethed because they only came to empty their bladders. The last few snowy weeks had produced more than ever. They dragged their disgusting children and tight-kneed wives past the priceless and sacred to seek only foul micturition in God's great temple. He could spot them a mile off and would turn the information board away from them, its plan of the abbey facing the wall. They would have to endure the humiliation of asking, after losing their direction amid the pews and chapels. He would wait for them at the raised eagle lectern. On its plinth he stood three feet higher than anybody else, virtuously consulting the vast Victorian Bible that nobody ever read from.

" 'Scuse, sir. Can you tell us where the WC is please?"

He ignored the yelping below and studiously consulted the permanently open pages.

"Please, sir. Where is the toilet?"

He roused his weary and distinguished eyes and peered down at the rabble below him. The shadow of the eagle and his glaring silhouette fell over them like a chilled conserve of guilt. Their urine was instantly staunched and no more questions were asked.

A similar party approached him two days later and told him about the "strange ol' monk". Their children greatly enjoying the tale and jumping about between the pews chirping, "Munky munky."

He glared at the sticky brats and hoped they might become petrified under his focus, when his lethal stare was interrupted by the woman of the party saying, "He's clergy, like yourself, sir. All dressed in a frock an' all."

Her husband elbowed her aside, seeing Chyme straightening his spine in a cobra-like arc of attack.

"She means he was wearing a hassock."

"Cassock," corrected Chyme in a venomous hiss.

"Anyroads, he says he ain't here."

"Good," said the Verger, who considered the matter closed.

Weighty

The High Street ran like a drunken serpent through Pulborough, and its houses, cottages, and pubs tried to cling to its speeding skin. It had once been the main coaching road between the coast and London, but that had been a long time ago. The road began at the foot of the great four-span bridge: a splendid contrivance of one of Brunel's more able apprentices. The muddy, weed-choked trickle that crept beneath it today was all that remained of the great Tysmundarum—a river famed in its importance and the density of its myth that once rivalled the Thames', and was significant before the Romans came. At the other end of the high street, it petered out into fields and tracks. Its stately memory ploughed out and splintered into different commercial needs. At its midpoint it became the fulcrum between the lychgate of the abbey and the stacked and collapsing façade of the Coach & Horses, the village's most significant secular building. Pilgrimage and business had always demanded that visitors to one must automatically become visitors to the other, such was their proximity and emphasis. The coaching inn was three hundred years old and boasted all manner of dignitaries and rogues as its prior customers. The last landlord but one had purchased "an original stagecoach" and had it permanently parked outside the inn, the authenticity of the bright yellow paint attracting much attention. The neat wooden carriage was in fact a Landau—half the size of the original mail coaches that once used the inn. Its modest elegance would scarcely hold four elegant customers, not the usual nine stalwarts of the sturdy, six horse "Mail Coach" that trundled over unmade roads for miserable hours upon end.

Pulborough had lost its value as a good stopover when the new road of 1845 bypassed it and headed straight to Great Tidings, the county's thriving market town.

There was no love lost between the abbey and the inn, and neither master believed in the purpose or meaning of the other.

William Penny ran the Coach & Horses like the surly captain of a dubiously credited ship. His staff would cling to the swelling sides of the ancient walls as he pulled his immense size through the public bar and into the saloon, like an exasperated cork escaping a nastily sphinctered bottle of sloe gin.

"Needs a good wipe," he growled beneath his boot-brush moustache. "A good wipe down."

One of the gaunt and colourless girls he so liked to employ skittered from behind the long wooden counter, cloth in hand, and began scrubbing at one of the low circular tables.

"So do I," he continued as he made a stabbing lunge at the barmaid's rear.

She quickly moved aside in a much practised Half Veronica that put the greasy table between them. She had seen his molestation telegraphed miles in advance of its action.

"Uncle Bill" was famous for his lecherous gropes. All his continually changing female staff had been victim to them. They were not of the subtle "Dead Hand" variety, where the perpetrator's absent-minded hand accidentally brushes against a delicate part of the female anatomy. Nor were they "cheeky slaps" or "affectionate pats". They were outright, undisguised snatches, the fingers curled for maximum grip or penetration. His daily attacks were mostly unsuccessful, but occasionally he managed to corner one of the new girls before the others had had time to warn her, inevitably sending her home bruised with tear stained eyes and a little extra cash for "overtime".

His much spoken claim to fame as a "godsend to the girls" was in direct opposition to his other claim of being the heaviest landlord in Britain: a title that remained un-refuted.

He tipped—or rather crushed—the scales at thirty-two stone. He was just over five-and-a-half feet tall, which meant that his great weight sat in a spherical mass that was always cleated and bound in a thick three-piece suit of smudged grey herringbone.

In his youth he had been a boxer, which had permanently installed a dainty speed to his small pointed feet. It also gave him the illusion of desirable manhood, a fantasy that only he possessed. It had been many a year since he had shared his nightly administrations with another human being, and sometimes because of the drink or the shrinkage in his arms he had difficulties locating the whereabouts of his splendour at all.

Mrs. Penny was long since gone, run off with a drayman who loaded her suitcase onto his cart as the last barrel of beer rolled off. The Coach & Horses started falling from grace the moment she left: the food slid out of wholesomeness into tired slackness, the only safe option being the bread and cheese; the guest rooms tumbled out of cosy into shabby; and the bars became silent and open at irregular times. The ancient coaching inn was near ruin when Maud Garner answered Uncle Bill's advert seeking a manager. A Stubb to his Ahab, and someone that he only ever touched up once.

The monk dared to set his sandaled toes in Uncle Bill's bar just as the first snow of the day had started to fall outside. The few who saw him said that he did not seem to understand how the pub worked and that it was only after ten minutes or so that he found his way to the counter and managed to order three pints of Ol' Stooky Bitter. Jenny, who was the newest and most nervous thin waif, carried the glasses to the table where the monk had finally seated himself. A small column of coins was awaiting her for payment. She snatched them up without giving offence and retreated to safety behind the counter. All the waifs were safe behind there—the narrow space prohibited any form of intimacy occurring. She was putting the coins in the cash register when she saw them more clearly. The sovereign's head was not the current king, nor was it any other she had ever seen before. She quickly took some of them into the kitchen, presenting them to Maudy (as she liked to be called by the girls and the customers, but never by Uncle Bill) with great apprehension, explaining that the old gentleman in the hassock had given 'em.

"Cassock," corrected Maudy while carrying them in her big pink hands to the waxy yellow light.

" 'T'aint foreign," she said, rotating what looked like a tyrant's head. "Can't make out the words."

She stepped away from Jenny, and now Alice had joined them to see what was going on. English pubs are not the places for unusual and perplexing occurrences. They rely on routine and calm, with the occasional exception on a Saturday night. So when the ears of oddity pricked up, it was sensed like a flutter throughout the establishment. She peered into the bar and saw the stranger seated at the table staring at the un-sipped beer as if he did not really understand its purpose.

"Poor ol' soul," she said. "They lives a 'ard life in those monasteries."

For Maudy had a heart of gold which glowed around anything to do with the Church, older folk, and small, large-eyed animals that did not bite. Its proportion of sentimentality was in contrast to the glassy organ that vindictively hid behind the shapeless bosom that confronted Uncle Bill with steely indifference every day of his working life. He cringed at the velocity of its inertia and kept well out of her allotted hours of management, which were bringing the customers and the money back again.

"We won't say nothing of it," she instructed the girls.

"But what if the gaffer finds out?" said Alice, biting her lip.

"Leave him to me."

And with that she turned away from the venerable monk as he lifted his glass. And from the other customers around him who quietly gnawed and sucked at the jelly of her hand-raised cold pork pies with a concentrated relish of enormous magnitude. She carried the ancient coins ceremoniously towards the cash register's gaping maw.

It would all have ended well there if the monk had not performed his abnormal—some say abominable—act.

Flinty

Montague Trilby was in his garden, under the tall trees whose crowns were raggedly bejewelled with dozens of rookeries. The birds were away about their daily business but he could still hear their calls circling the branches over the buffeting icy wind. He liked this land and its pagan parishes that had existed for thousands of years—the creaking night woods listening from the summits of the forlorn hills. He tried to walk every day, as much to avoid the squabbles and petty nuisance of his parishioners as to taste the pleasures of the landscape. He was thinking of leaving the vicarage garden and climbing Saxonbury Tor, the most dramatic of the Iron Age swellings which surrounded the abbey. He contemplated the delight of the prospect for a few seconds more than he should have—a few seconds in which his vision and his escape were trashed. The squeaking gate announced the arrival of his least favourite goat of his most peculiar flock.

"Canyun Muntagrew," she squawked. "Iyve cuman see yous abowt the nuwd ghoust in the church."

At the age of eighty-nine most people become a little confused about the reality of their lives, and their ways of expressing themselves become a little shaky and indistinct. But Annabelle Chert had always talked like that, weirder than any other member of the village and indeed those few who were said to be members of her disjointed family. Every acrid syllable gurned and every mispronunciation grated against the Canon's subtle mind.

"Cos itwaynt one of ouws."

He stood speechless looking down at the tiny woman, who seemed to be dressed in her night gown and Wellington boots under the thick and stained donkey jacket that she always wore.

"Ours," he said, the collective pronoun sounding like rancid ashes.

"Ihm frun elsweerns."

"Mmm," was all he could manage.

"Wulls, whyts yuus gunna dues abowwit?"

"I am sorry, Mrs. Chert, but I don't quite underst—"

"He's awruungen."

She had, of course, gone to Verger Chyme first, but he had had little time for her incomprehensible rambles. Groups of visitors were arriving, still in ignorance of their need of his erudition and knowledge of the great building. The last thing they should be subjected to was the superstitious garbage of this unsanitary old witch.

"I suggest you go home now, Mrs. Chert. I am rather busy."

"Byssy myarrse."

"There is no need for that kind of language in God's house," he declared.

"Thens yoous ahear whats Iamms asayyin or Isel go tellon the Canyon immself."

"An excellent idea, Madam."

And with that he hurried to catch his next crop of victims for the privilege of his full historic tour.

Chert and Chyme were the good Canon's curse: mirror image demons put amongst us to taunt and harry all that is kind and generous. Pitch-forked harpies made manifest to test his faith and his patience with the less than perfect world. At least they counterbalanced each other to achieve a kind of equilibrium that allowed him a space to ignore both. But that was before the third demon arrived from London.

Beery

Uncle Bill was in the public bar at a table with a swag of his cronies, regular drinkers, trustworthy yeomen of the hop. He couldn't have seen what had happened in the other bar, his gigantic back facing its entrance. Nor did he see anything on the limpid faces of the men before him as he was berating them on the subject of the dangers of learning. And nothing of sound made him ponderously swivel the bastion of his body around.

'Twas not the dull clucking like so many leaden hens of the unknown coins falling on and escaping across the flagstone floor that reached his ear, and poor Jenny's startled whelp never dared stretch so far. It was that shiver of out-of-place-ness mentioned before. The untoward let loose for a second or two to thrill the stiff and stagnant air.

Billy turned and steered towards it, his bulk gliding on a righteous wave of purpose. He reached the door as the third pint was finished and the monk gently put his glass down on the table in the silent room. Everybody had stopped eating and talking. Behind the counter Alice had covered her mouth with her hand, and further back behind her Maudy slowly crossed herself. The pool under the monk's wet sandaled feet was still growing as it dripped from his heavy robe. Billy's eyes flickered back and forth from the monk's face to the row of empty glasses and then to the puddle beneath him. Back and forth, back and forth in time with the pendulum of the grandfather clock that stood against the far wall.

"You dirty fucker," he growled, then he charged through the narrow passage, smearing framed pictures off the wall and sending the other customers and their lunches spilling in all directions.

"Soil my house, would ya?"

His big broken pink fist clutched handfuls of the cassock's morbid cloth and lifted it out of the chair as if it were no more than a paper bag. So unexpected was his colossal strength or the emptiness of the other man's weight that he brought the monk up high in the room, above his head and crashing into the wooden chandelier, bringing it, and a hail of plaster and stucco, down. Everybody flinched back and protected their eyes as Uncle Bill regained his breath and rage and continued to bully and kick the flailing blur of the monk out of the bar, through the shouting hall and into the snow-covered road. He was pleased with the potency of his manliness, especially at his age. It had been a good many years since he had given anyone a good thrashing. He stood above the sprawling figure with drool on his chin and triumph cresting his anger. All the light fluttering snow shrivelled in the aura of his red glow, making him radiant in the cold white air.

"I don't care who or what you are, holy man or saint. No one soils my pub in such a disgusting way. Don't they teach you no common decency in them convents of yours?"

The snow was falling more heavily now and Billy had to wipe it off his thick moustache and balding pate, the back of his hand wiping his bleary eyes so that he could see the fallen man.

Everybody in the pub was still as the world around it swirled. Only one customer and Alice had gone to the windows to watch more closely. The rest sat or stood frozen in shock, or something else. It was getting really cold now and the flakes had changed their consistency: no longer wafting weightless petals without directions or care, but icier, more solid particles with a purpose and speed. Billy felt his skeleton shiver for the first time in a long while, deep inside its meaty cladding.

"Be off," he shouted into the snow white road and strode back into his domain, trying not to slip and ruin the effect of his eminence.

That afternoon turned into a wild night in the Coach & Horses. William Penny's cronies hailed him as a hero. He brought a bottle of whisky to their table to show his appreciation. The patrons who'd witnessed the affray were apologised to by Maudy, who got the waifs to repair and tidy the room while she gave customers tea and brandy and offered rooms for the night to save them from the storm outside. On the house, of course. Alice had to be told to come away from the window three times before she finally did.

"Come on, girl, we need you," said Maudy stiffly. Then she saw the girl's expression and waited.

"He never got up."

"Are you sure?"

"I been looking all along."

"Get your coat."

Maudy had taken command again and she steered the girl into the passage and out towards the servants' entrance. They put on boots and top coats and went outside.

"Just a couple of minutes to make sure," said Maudy, pulling her headscarf tighter against the snow. She had picked up a walking stick from the lost collection that sprouted from the hall stand. They were arm in arm with heads down against the buffeting snow as they approached the place where Alice said the monk had fallen. The snow was about four inches deep on the uneven road and they peered through the storm until they saw the mound.

"There he be," said Alice in a frightened voice, stopping dead in her tracks with her bony arms now rigid in Maudy's embrace.

Slowly the older woman stepped away from the shivering girl and pointed the stick before her, tapping the gentle snow. Alice had both her hands over her mouth when the stick probed the mound and passed through it. Maudy waved its tip inside the hump, dispersing its form into flatness. She turned her scarfed, flapping face back to the girl.

"It's all right, lass. There's nothing there."

"Thanks, Maudy," said Alice. "It must have been the snow; he must have buggered off in the snow."

The older woman said nothing and looked into her tea. It was warm, female, and safe in the kitchen. Jenny was at the sink finishing the washing up.

"I still don't understand why the guv'nor got so cross," she said distractedly.

"What?" said Alice, amazed. "He got 'cross' cause the nasty ol' bugger pissed all over the floor."

"Did he? I thought he just spilt it."

"What, three pints? That's a lot of bloody spillin'."

Maudy poured more tea from the big earthen-coloured pot.

"Perhaps he was sick?" said Jenny after much thought. "What you think, Maudy?"

Maudy put her cup down and looked at both girls in turn.

"It weren't spilt and he didn't wee. It just went straight through him."

"How?"

" 'Cause he wasn't all there."

"What, mental-in-the-head you mean?"

"No, not all there in a living sense. Not a living man's body," she said quietly, crossing herself again.

Oily

Maudy Garner's letter sat unopened with others on Walter Prince's great laboratory table, while he and a young woman held hands. Her hands were fastened by permanent leather straps attached to the mahogany surface with brass screws. She was also blindfolded, and he never took his eyes off of her. An electric cable ran from its controls next to Prince's notebook and pipe, down across the table to where she sat at its edge. It curled to the floor then crept up the girl's right leg where it disappeared up and under her skirts. A series of jolts or quivers could be detected by small regular movement under the soft material of her tight mask and also in her fingertips. Prince would occasionally let go of one of her hands to make pencil notes on a jotting pad, before increasing the voltage a notch or two.

"Wery good, my dear. Try to relax against the current, absorb its sensation."

She grimaced and closed her eyes under the cloth and said nothing. Prince adjusted the second knob on the desk, the one marked "F" for frequency. Her flickering evolved into a tiny shimmer that had extended outwards into her shoulders, hips and ankles. There was also a change in her breathing.

"Wery good," he congratulated himself as he sucked on his long, protruding front teeth.

Another of his experiments was working. This one testing the emotional reflexes of a paid female sitter. He watched with polished scientific distance as he manipulated her physical reactions, which he had so ingeniously separated from the selfish whims of individual emotional needs that normally operated such responses, especially female ones, which he found had always proved to be fickle and disappointingly irregular. If desires and the other intimate mechanisms could be calibrated and controlled thus, then he might be halfway to regulating the more complex sensations of mediums and clairvoyance. He watched her mouth carefully, teasing the "M" for magnitude control a little higher before reaching back to feel all her fingers again. The agitation there was most convincing. He almost made another note, but decided to hold on to her pinkies just a little longer. After heightening the frequency again he was considering changing the knobs for a foot pedal to keep his hands free—the kind of thing that the new electric sewing machines used to control their speed—when a knocking came to his door.

"Bother," he said under his breath.

Prince had indeed learnt to become a civilised and cultured man. "Bother" was not part of the vocabulary that he had grown up with in South East London. The use of that word there, amongst his juvenile peers would have promoted outrage, scorn, and physical violence. The allowed and encouraged expletives of the Old Kent Road would have sent the shivering young lady fleeing from the experiment and his company. If she had understood them at all. His latest batch of "volunteers" had all been immigrant workers from Yugoslavia and Hungary. Their interest in furthering knowledge often seemed as great as their need to obtain unofficial donations of cash, and after an initial "breaking in" some became willing and almost polite.

"Yes, coming," he called and grabbed his pipe off the bench, accidentally clicking three more notches on the "F" knob.

He unbolted the door and allowed a three inch gap.

"Telegram, sir," said the faithful Miss Wainscoot.

Prince snatched the proffered paper waving in the gap and shut the door quickly. He looked up for a moment across his long bent nose but did not really see what the girl was doing. He tore open the paper as she rhythmically bucked against the restraints. Her previous expression of anxiety had been wafted away and now the visible part of her face and the rest of her body were caressed in a growing undulation that looked not unlike pleasure. He had the telegram in his hand.

"By Jove," he exclaimed. "Astonishing!"

Little sounds of anguish were escaping his subject's lips.

"I must confirm—"

He darted for the door and then stopped.

"Oopsy-daisy, I nearly forgot," he said, almost in time with her soft panting.

He quickly flicked the off switch and the machine instantly stopped, retracting all its stimulus and jolting the girl into reality, much in the same way as a conjuror does when with a great flourish he yanks a tablecloth away, leaving all the plates and glasses, forks and spoons, and other occupants still intact on the bare board.

"Won't be a mo'," he explained before making his exit, leaving the door wide open on the lost girl.

The conversation was less than he might have expected, having come from so high an' all. The Scientific Society for Psychical Research was Prince's own baby: a one-man band disguised as, and with the ambitions of, a symphony orchestra. Its board of governors was made up of eminent names whom he had coerced into giving him their credibility. Minor aristocracy, pauper princes of the church, military failures, obscure academics, and a Scottish industrialist who had been a third cousin removed to the recently late Sir Arthur Conan Doyle. Most of them would have been burnt at the stake a few hundred years earlier or confined to the Hogarthian wards of Bedlam. None had money, much to Prince's chagrin. Not even Donald MacTavish, laird of his clan and inventor of the propelling ink pen, a seemingly ingenious idea that followed on from his great success with the "Claymore", a rubber cartridge fountain pen made for the masses, and the "Wee Robbie" propelling lead pencil. But the "Sir Walter" was an innovation too far and went into production without being thoroughly tested. Its originality was a sprung plunger that automatically pushed the ink in the barrel forwards to the nib, thus giving the pen the ability to write against gravity. It was decided to make it a handsome, deluxe icon to rival the handcrafted pens of Germany that had long held the upper market as fashionable objects of desire. So pleased was MacTavish with its design that he changed its name to the "Ben Nevis" and put all of his normally cautious wealth behind the project. A vast publicity campaign had been planned by canny folk in Edinburgh and London, and the re-calibrated machines of his factory in Fife began to roll in time to hit the eagerly awaiting market just before Christmas. The campaign was a huge success. The pen sold like hot cakes. It was hurriedly bought up by those that could afford such a luxury and a few thousand who could not. Its elegant box showed Sir Walter, the great man of letters, at ease in cave or a broch, somewhere in the Highlands. He sprawled fully kilted on his back, composing another masterpiece, his notebook held aloft, pressing against the cave's craggy roof. In his hand the famed pen exquisitely calligraphed his noble thought, upside down. The pen became a status symbol by Boxing Day. Kings, Emperors, and Prime Ministers bought them. Oriental Potentates purchased them by the crate to gift their loyal slaves and concubines. It was a new must have among those who had everything else.

Alas! By Hogmanay horrible rumours had begun to spread. The "Ben Nevis" had certainly proved its ability to write upside down as all those that owned one had proved to their friends and loved ones over the holidays. Unfortunately, its performance in the normal mode was less than satisfactory. After the festivities were over, the pen was taken into the real world, where it was meant to impress all those who saw it sign contracts, ceremonial charters, death certificates, and state documents of austere solemnity. Unexpectedly, the added suction of gravity so excited the spring and nib that the pen began to flow with great abandon when held upright, depositing the entire contents of its barrel onto the shy documents below in long unstoppable emissions. Not to mention the woeful despoilment of the Sultan of Kashmir's bride-to-be's white wedding gown. The sultan had told his emir to fill the august instrument with red ink to gain the most splendid effect. The effect on the virgin's dress was considered far from splendid and the outrage caused a diplomatic incident of a grave nature, the irate sultan declaring war on Scotland. The pen's terrible gushes were the signature of MacTavish's demise. Bankruptcy followed a flurry of lawsuits in the New Year and by Easter his factory had closed. It was said that his workers stood cap in hand, tears in eyes as he left the premises for the last time.

This of course removed any hope of the Scot being the major benefactor of Prince's SSPR. So now he was seeking a patron elsewhere. The voice on the telephone belonged to Audwin Blatty, a celebrated poet of the Fitzrovia Chaise Longue School. It was he who had sent the telegram, indicating that his soirée of associates was interested in doing something "novel" with the supernatural. Prince knew that a few of this inner circle were famed for their enormous wealth and boredom, and he anxiously exchanged the telephone from hand to hand in damp excitement at the prospect. A meeting was to be arranged at his convenience.

"Yes, yes, certainly."

The call was going swimmingly until the final furlong.

"Ah! One other thing. Do you know the attractive Hamlet of Pulborough, Mr. Prince?"

"Pulborough?"

"Ye-es, in the county of Lower Kent."

"Well, yes, I have heard of i-it."

Prince stuttered for the first time in the call. Telephones are instruments of torture for the stutterer, racks that agonisingly extend and tear the spaces between trapped words and the impatience of the speaker at the other end. Often, when a word is jammed in the hideous place between the mind and the voice, the only sounds that escape are little hisses and clucks that the listener miles away can only understand as a faulty line, and thus they feel the need to interrupt and make things worse.

"Hello? Hello? Something's wrong here."

Locked, clenched ghosts of words.

"Hello? It's the bloody line."

"No-o i-i-it's my ssst-t-t—"

"Hello? There's some kind of fault on the line."

"No, i-i-it's m-m-my . . . "

"No good, we will have to try later."

"W-w-wai—"

"Goodbye."

Prince had suffered like so many others until he developed his own technique. It was a kind of modified sneer, where his lips, followed by his mouth, would climb around the outside of his protruding teeth, much in the same way that a mountaineer stealthily transverses a curved outcrop of rock. He had discovered this unique ability when undergoing his gruelling elocution lessons.

"*Hello?*" said Blatty.

"Yes, it's not far from my country residence."

"Good."

For a moment both men had forgotten the thrust of their conversation. Then Blatty picked it up.

"There are strange goings-on down there. Apparitions in the Abbey, that sort of thing. Distant cousin of mine wrote me about it, and you."

"Me?"

"Said she had sent you a letter weeks ago."

There was a pause in which the accusation and the challenge were balanced.

"I will talk to my secretary about it, she is rather slip-shod sometimes."

A considerable amount of spittle had gathered around Prince's last words and he quickly swabbed it on the shoulder pad of his tweed jacket before continuing.

"What would your cousin like me to do?"

"Distant cousin."

"Quite."

"It would be interesting to see what you made of it all?"

"Yes, I see."

"Her name is Maud Garner, she can be found at the Coach & Horses Inn, opposite the entrance to the abbey."

"Is she the proprietor?"

"Something like that . . . "

"I will contact her tomorrow."

"Excellent, do tell me the outcome and then we can fix those dates."

"Of course."

"Good day."

"Good day."

Prince lit his pipe on his way back to the laboratory, thinking that the task he had just been given sounded as dull as dish water. Another ghost monk in another abbey. Two-a-penny and never any evidence or proof. He noticed the letters on the desk and probed them with the wet mouthpiece of his pipe until he saw the Pulborough postmark. He retrieved it and slit it open with a switchback knife that he always kept about his person.

The handwriting was neat but uneducated and said nothing more than he had already been told. The letter declared itself from the Coach & Horses. Ah! Well, better get it over and done with. He screwed the letter up into a ball and threw it across the room in the direction where his subject had been strapped to the bench. It was only then that he noticed that she was gone. She had left without his permission, a rude act of ingratitude which she must have enlisted help in. Somebody needed to have undone the straps.

"Wainscoot!" he bellowed beyond the confines of his ordered world, somewhere into the chaos and foolishness of the exterior universe.

Blasphemy

Canon Trilby stood in the central aisle, scratching his head. The monk had been seen again and for some unknown reason Verger Chyme was now taking the matter seriously.

He stood beside the thin lofty priest, looking up at the noble man's bewildered amusement with growing distaste. He pointed again at the empty pews.

"He was seen there, midway in the Pillock pew."

Trilby scratched the other side of his head and let his watery eyes drift in the general direction of the nicotine-stained finger. Even after all these years in the abbey he could not remember the names of all of the sponsored family pews, hymn books, choir robes and other "gifts" that wilfully nailed the existence of local minor dynasties into the fabric and history of the great church. The Pillocks were pig farmers who had been bolted into the parish since Cromwell had favoured them for their staunch support. Grim unsmiling folk who seemed to miss the excitement of their forebear's carnage, and now only miserably acted it out on their livestock. The Pillocks resisted anything modern, ornate or decorated. A stoic lime-washed plainness stiffened all their inflexible blood.

It was the only common feature that the troublesome clan still shared. The pew was solid oak, purposely unvarnished and only polished by the generations of swine-bloated rears. Even Old Mary Vanes and her daughter were banned from using "products" to clean its deeply grained surface.

"I don't really see what we are to do," the Canon said wistfully.

"Put a stop to it, that's what."

"Um, ban him, you mean?"

"Exorcise it."

Trilby jolted like one stumbling on a shallow step in a deep dream. He re-focussed on the small man beneath him as if seeing him for the first time.

"You have seen it, Cedric?"

Chyme did not flinch from the lofty man's enquiring eyes.

"Yes, Canon. I was showing some visitors the chancel yesterday when I heard it. The pews had been empty as we passed them by. Empty and in bright sunlight. When I heard it I turned around and saw the shadow in the glare . . . and heard the voice."

"What was it saying?"

"It was laughing a prayer."

There was a silence between the men; both had broken their gaze on each other and were now looking at the row of stiff pews. As if prompted, sun filled the west window and made the wood glow and passively declare its timeless corporality. Dust motes swam languidly in the settling air.

"What exactly do you mean, Cedric, laughing a prayer?"

"I think it was the Quicunque Vult of the Morning Prayer, but it was difficult to tell because of the laughing."

"The Creed of Saint Athanasius?"

"Just part of it, over and over again:

" 'Such as the Father is,

" 'Such is the Son: and such is the Holy Ghost.

" 'The Father uncreate

" 'The Son uncreate: and the Holy Ghost uncreate.

" 'The Father incomprehensible,

" 'The Son incomprehensible: and the Holy Ghost

" 'Incomprehensible.' "

A cloud passed over the sun and the pews shrank back as the church swallowed its volume.

"Over and over again."

"You saw and heard this?"

"Yes, sir. As God is my witness."

"Did you approach it?"

"No," said Chyme in a voice that neither man had heard before.

A silence grew in the air around them while the clouds, unlistening, passed the sun. This was not the rigid, difficult man that had dominated the abbey for years. The unquestioning dedication and the self-righteous pride had evaporated. Chyme's exoskeleton of pompous permafrost had melted before him, revealing a small lost question mark hanging beneath the Canon's assessment. Then Trilby, as if to break the tension and give back some authority, said:

"Did the others you were escorting hear or see anything?"

"No, I don't think so."

"Don't you know, didn't you ask them?"

A glimmer of Chyme spite found its way back to rectify his salvation.

"They were outsiders, nobodies. They looked like they saw and understood nothing."

"I see," declared the Canon.

Chyme heard the crystals of doubt and blame grind in Trilby's cautious exclamation and it stiffened him enough to shiver off his vulnerability and become a couple of inches taller.

"I know this place better than any. I have given my life to its very fabric, as well as its sacred purpose."

Anger was now at his well and it was working hard to hoist back bucketsful of heavy venomous hubris.

"I take this matter very seriously and intend to demand an appropriate response, even if I have to go to the

Bishop myself."

Trilby was taken aback by the sudden ferocity of the little man's vehemence and the way it seemed to be turning into a personal attack.

"Cedric, nobody is underestimating what you are saying."

"I won't have that. *Not* under any circumstances and from nobody."

The "and that includes you" was not said but implied as if written in stone.

"Cedric, Cedric, please contain yourself. Let's talk quietly in my office."

And before another word was said the wise Canon softly turned and made his way with an exaggerated, dignified slowness towards the cloister door.

Snowy

Prince arrived in Pulborough on a Saturday morning as the snow was melting. The car from the station dropped him in the slushy road between the abbey and the inn, next to the yellow stagecoach. He swung his feet out of the unheated interior of the cab and stepped into six inches of soaking slush. What he said to the unpopulated street was an invective from the core of his origin, untouched by any cosmetic politeness. He was thinking that he should have driven himself, brought the "Rolls" to impress the yokels. It had only been the dismal weather that had prevented him from cruising through the counties in his cherished limousine.

It was obvious that the taxi driver was not going to budge an inch, so Prince heaved his heavy case from the vehicle, reluctantly paid, and struggled towards the entrance, losing his footing and skidding painfully into the splits. He quickly grabbed out to save himself and caught hold of the cold brass handle of the stagecoach door which was solidly welded closed: Penny's solution to a previous incident some years before with local youths.

He pulled against it and rectified himself, desperately hoping that nobody inside the inn had seen such an undignified arrival. The coach sighed and then creaked, and grudgingly rocked against its rusted and painted-over springs. Prince was thinking about what to do next when one of Billy's waifs appeared at the door. His relief at seeing her was instantly replaced by the fear of appalling embarrassment. Because in the few seconds under his connoisseur gaze, he had seen her comeliness glow through the thin translucence of her peasant skin and the slouch of her raw-boned stance. He had a long and successful track record with such creatures. They had been drawn to his suave urbanity and cultured masculinity and he had helped them release their trapped womanly potential.

"Good morning, my dear. I was just admiring your fine vehicular antique, eighteenth century if I am not mistaken?"

Jenny said nothing, but just stared at him. Charming, he thought. A rabbit in the headlights, delightfully caught in the potency of his cobra-like gaze. Indeed, Jenny did seem mesmerised by the man holding onto the door of the awkwardly rocking coach, or rather by something just above and beyond him. She slowly raised her thin nervous arm to point over his head. Delightful! He thought her breath had been taken away. Prince was just about to give her a devastating compliment so that she might help him and carry his heavy luggage inside, when the entire mass of snow and wet ice that had accumulated on the roof of the stagecoach slid sideways and languidly fell on his head.

Nosey

Annabelle Chert was the last of her line, and the shame of it had brutalised her life.

The Cherts had been the oldest occupants of Pulborough, their ragged but adamant line adhering to the banks of the diminishing Tysmundarum no matter what. Little Anna had been an ugly child who grew aggressively into an ugly woman. Courtship of any kind seemed illusionary and she showed little interest in the opposite sex. It was her aunts that found the Werricks' blind son Albert as a possible suitor. Annabelle barely had a say in it. They married in the summer of 1901 at the abbey, on a grey lifeless day of her thirty-second year. All the Cherts had married there, since some of them had helped carry the stones that made it. Mr. and Mrs. Werricks' life together was troublesome and erratic, and when it became clear that she was "burren" it expanded their mutual disinterest until they barely spoke. Young Albert died in the great flu epidemic and she lived alone for the rest of her days. A year after he had gone she took back her maiden name, seeing no point in answering to one she had never really been.

Over the following decades Annabelle became the sole surviving Chert and took on a great responsibility for the abbey and its ghosts, some of which might have been her "ayncessors". Her care grew in direct proportion to her vanishing clan, so that now in her "wys olage" she was not going to be fobbed off by those "Wippitnakers" who now ran "her" church. She and her kin had been stalwarts of its proper meaning for centuries. They all knew that its foundation by Saint Ercrat the Benign was meant to keep the forces of darkness at bay: the elder brooding forces that existed in all the unnamed mounds and half-ploughed hillocks; those that were worshipped by pagan tribes in the spinneys and copses atop every significant hill. The abbey had been established to ward off the influence of the largest—Saxonbury Tor itself, which all knew was really called Saxonbury's Knob. It was up there that Ercrat had preached his first sermon, his feet still encrusted with the mud of his journey up the river valley and into their fold.

The great church grew there to be close to the people and help them not to go astray. The generations of monks who came to live there all understood its purpose and worked and prayed ceaselessly to keep the engine of its influence broadcasting over the haunted fields. When the king sent the monks away and broke all the pictures and bleached all the colour in the abbey, a great shadow came off of the hill and slithered into the valley and the simple hearts of the people. She knew all of this because her parents had told her, as had their parents before, and theirs before, and theirs before.

She had seen the monks going to and fro in her younger days, but they had grown more transparent over the years until only a wisp of their passing remained. But that was all right, it was the natural way. Her mother had told her so and she had grown accustomed to not seeing them anymore. That's what had alarmed her about the new one who had turned up sitting in the pews. "Etwernt natrul", being so "sulid anall".

So she decided to track this "nuen", and that's when she became really alarmed. It had been a game when she was young, her and her brothers and cousins. "Muncspyin", they had called it. They would wait around the abbey in a loose pack until one was seen, then would whistle to each other and close in to quietly stalk their prey, keeping a considerable distance and following all the convolutions of the ghosts' paths until they faded. She did the same now and had watched the "nuen" in the pew, heard him chuckling out prayers in a way she had never heard before and never cared to again. There was something deeply "wruung" with this one. She had followed him out into the churchyard and spied upon him reading the names of the dead on the weathered stones, then followed him further into the twilight woods at the edge of the hallowed ground, where the others were buried. That's where she lost him. One minute clear in the trees, the next minute gone. She had waited as the light faded and the rooks gathered in the freezing branches. She grew weary and turned back on her steps, then she saw it, on the glimmering ground: two tracks of footprints in the snow. Her own deep twisted impressions and another, bigger but lighter as if no weight had been applied to their making. Distinctive sandal prints running in line with hers. The figure she had followed out of the yellow candlelight and into blue evening was much bigger than she—a good six feet and more she reasoned, and bulky too. But these prints were made with the touch of a feather. Her blood ran cold in the chill air. Ghosts had no prints at all. Men, big men, had deep ones. This was something else, something wrong: "Awruungen".

She knew that no one would believe her and that no matter how loud she shouted, they all would remain deaf to her alarm. She was walking home muttering under her billowing breath, ignoring the looks from the strangers in the village and retreating rapidly to her cottage under the bridge next to the babbling stream. In her garden between the gate and her front door was a spindly bird table, where earlier that morning she had put a few scraps of bacon rind and the knob end of a hard, stale loaf of bread. As she passed its lopsided, frosted surface something gleamed at her. Ice, she thought as she rummaged in her pockets for her keys. Then she stopped dead. Not ice. She returned to the table. Every scrap of the leftovers was gone, not even a crumb remained. The only thing that occupied the square wooden plateau was a coin, a quaint and heavy one. She removed one of her mittens and tried to pick it up, but it was frozen to the surface. She dug her horny nails around it and levered it away. It was old, unknown, but contained the cold dead weight of value. She stepped back in puzzlement, her foot cracking a frozen puddle of ice. She looked down at its bright reflection and saw the shadow in its surface and the signs in the snow either side of it. Wide, even prints of sandals that weighed less than the frozen coin clenched in her other mittened hand.

Smokey

"The new gent was none too pleased, Maudy," said Alice who had been awaiting the elder woman's return.

She was carrying large bags of groceries and seemed pleased to be back in the inn.

"Why's that?"

" 'Cause a quantity of snow fell on him outside. Fair ruined his hat, he said."

"Never mind, I will soon have him to rights."

"Said he came for you he did."

Maudy stopped fussing with the bags.

"Oh my word, weren't Mr. Prince, were it?"

"Yes, Maudy, that's what he wrote in the book."

"Oh my word."

"Wrote it big and loud and scrawly like."

"Oh my word, where is he now?"

"In the bar, warming up, he said."

Maudy put the bags down and nodded to Jenny to take them into the kitchen. She then adjusted her hair and her dress and made her way towards the sound of men. To her horror, Prince was engaged in conversation with Uncle Billy. This was the last thing she had wanted. The old publican would sour the pitch, good and proper. They sat at the far end of the snug, both leaning across a small circular table, talking head to head, smoke to smoke. Both gnawed at their gushing pipes: Billy's a curved, hanging, knobbly question mark of a pipe that hugged the contours of his massive face, while Prince sported a strait briar that stabbed out from his protruding teeth and hawk-like nose. Great lungfuls of smoke and a chain of drinks had bound the men together. What they were saying or what they had in common was unimaginable. Maudy watched them and waited for her moment. It came when both their pipes burnt out and each man reloaded with his favourite plug. For Billy it was Condor, a rich tarry tobacco, black and always moist, somewhere between plum pudding and leather. Prince preferred the more sophisticated, tweedy blend of Balkan Sorbraini, with its perfume of distinguished Empire Latakya.

Billy eyed Wally's white circular can with controlled disapproval, the gaily coloured tobacco nestling inside an immaculate ruff of crisp paper. It's what in any other circumstances he would have called "a poof's smoke".

Both men had recharged and were tamping the tobacco down into the bowls of their pipes, Billy with a thumb that he had previously dipped in his whisky, when Maudy presented herself at their table and coughed and announced her name. Billy gave her a cursory glance from the scrum of the masculine conversation. Prince looked her up and down, registering disappointment, and then reluctantly he began to stand to pay her the minimum of politeness that was due. Billy grabbed the sleeve of his suit and dragged him back into his seat.

"Gent here says he come to see you. Says you been writing to him about things that go bump in the night, right here in *my* pub."

Price settled his gaze on his large whisky before him.

"That's correct, Mr. Penny, we do have business together."

"Oh! Business is it? There was me thinking it was all hogwash gossip about that disgusting old priest that pissed his hassock."

"Cassock," Prince corrected quietly.

"Hassock, cassock, whatever it was, he pissed in it."

Maudy did not care for his tone, his language or his innuendoes and her wrinkled face displayed it.

"*Well?*" barked Billy.

"I think we saw the incident differently," she stated coldly.

"Bloody right we did," guffawed Billy.

"I think it best if Mr. Prince and I have our own conversation."

"Bloody good idea," sneered Billy. "When we have finished ours I will send him over to you."

And with that Billy turned back to his pint and chaser and lit his pipe while starting to address Prince as if there was nobody else in the room. She had been dismissed and left the men, hiding her seething rage.

Billy did not let Prince go until both men were incoherent. Maudy went about her daily business but kept one eye on the door of the snug, waiting to apologise and catch the great man when he retreated. However, a growing doubt about Prince was occurring with each hour he spent seemingly happily with Penny's conversation. Occasionally they would both roar with laughter or cup their heads together in clandestine whispers. Finally she saw signs of blurred movement in the smog of their tobacco.

"Got to vwisit the lidle boys' room," slurred Billy, his chair screeching as he pushed it backwards.

"I 'spect *she'll* be awaiting on you, in need of your services."

He winked loudly and cast his red bloated gaze randomly down through all the bars, hoping that it might grubbily bruise Maudy, wherever she was. He then grinned and stumbled sideways into the cringing passageway.

Maudy confronted Prince as he steadied himself up the wooden staircase to his room.

"I am slorry, miss. I-I-I have had a tiring journey and a bothersome arrival and now fleel inneed of a liddel siesta. I look fwoward to spleaking later."

And with that he scanned the distant peak, sucked in a deep wet breath and began his ascent.

Gassy

He never appeared again that day and she decided she would not brood on his rudeness till after church. Best not to carry such grievances into God's house on a holy day. The abbey was bustling with mild warmth as she came in out of the cold eastern wind that had risen up at dawn. People were unwrapping their scarves and pulling off their hats in the vestibule. Old Darius Munt was stamping his frozen feet so noisily that even he could hear them thawing. The rest of the congregation were picking up prayer books and selecting their favourite pews. A general good-natured hum was gathering itself from all their softly spoken conversations and greetings. Maudy went to her normal place in the third pew from the front and made herself comfortable while awaiting the arrival of poor old Mrs. Chert. They always sat together because Maudy was one of the very few who would tolerate her presence and the rich manners of her undiluted rural life. She was normally there first, impatiently waiting for everyone else after she had made her inspection of the building. She had never been absent before, even in the thickest of winters. It was even said that she had attended Sunday communion while her husband died slowly all those years before. By the time everybody was seated and the organ wheezed into life, Maudy's concern had turned into pure anxiety. The tiny choir followed the rigid Verger as he carried the cross through the church, Canon Trilby walking behind, smiling and clearly enjoying the highlight of his professional week.

It was Quinquagesima Sunday—fifty days before Easter and three before Ash Wednesday—and this only served to emphasise the old lady's absence because she always paid great attention to this week, often wearing the ash for days in advance and retreat of the actual day. Last year she had caused a great peck of trouble by arriving at the Sunday service with the traditional, and long since obsolete, mark of the ashes on her forehead. This would have been ignored if her application of it had followed the usual reserved daub. But Mrs. Chert must have got carried away in repentance. She looked as if she had burrowed her head in the grate of a long-dead fire. Her entire head and hair were clogged with ash and bits of cindered wood as she strode through the church, her normal painful slouched transmogrified into a stately stride. Wisps of dust and ashes drifted off her countenance like celestial smoke as she passed through the silenced congregation.

The service continued and Maudy found she was distracted. She looked behind and around her during the hymns, while everybody else concentrated on their reading of the words and the discordance of their voices. Even Darius Munt's singing—unsettlingly loud and one line behind everybody else—did not involve her, even when it creaked out after the rest had fallen silent, as Canon Trilby mounted the steps of the pulpit in a glow of amiable confidence. With great relish and a timbre that had been honed against amateur dramatics during his time in the seminary, he resoundingly launched into his reading of St. Paul's First Epistle to the Corinthians:

"*Though* I speak with the tongues of men and of angels, and have not charity, I am become as sounding brass, or a tinkling cymbal. And though I have the gift of prophecy, and understand all mysteries, and all knowledge; and though I have all faith, so that I could remove mountains, and have not charity, I am nothing. And though I bestow all my goods to feed the poor, and though I give my body to be burned, and have not charity, it profiteth me nothing . . . "

He mistakenly paused a moment to let the clarity of his voice and the portent of its meaning carry though the abbey. He was just about to launch into, "Charity suffereth long," when the first giggle sounded and everyone turned to look at the Pillock pew. Only five of the assorted Pillocks sat there, with much space between them.

Pamela and her husband John Larkin sat on the outside and stared inward towards Wilfred, his wife Nancy and their adolescent son Giles, who stared back from their positions nested close to the north wall. They were all looking at the absent space between them, the very spot where the monk had been seen before. The giggling had stopped, but the taste of it hung in the air, accusingly near the Pillocks. Chyme had sprung to his feet and was craning his neck to see who had perpetrated the outrage. Up in his box Canon Trilby cleared his throat and continued the lesson in a slightly more subdued tone.

"Charity suffereth long, and is kind; charity envieth not; charity vaunteth not itself, is not puffed up . . . "

The next sound came from inside the pulpit itself and was of a rude and vulgar nature. All the eyes that were already on Trilby blinked and dared not look away. He turned around in the confined space, examining all around him as if looking for a misplaced item rather than the source of a sound. A light and unusual anger was beginning to tint the normally sallow complexion of the genial priest, and it was being mixed with a new sensation that others would recognise as embarrassment—all stirred together in the high box of wood that held him isolated above the sea of eyes.

He returned to the Bible and held the lectern tight as he began to read. He started the next verse, not wanting to continue with the former that had been so horribly sullied. But some part of his mind was in turmoil. Who would dare play this nasty little joke on him? Which one of those below was enjoying his humiliation? He unreeled the faces of the possible perpetrators while still reading solemnly.

"Charity never faileth: but whether there be prophecies, they shall fail; whether there be tongues, they shall cease . . . "

Then an even worse thought occurred. Supposing he had imagined it, imagined it all, and the poor innocents below had heard nothing but only witnessed his strange behaviour? Supposing the horrid noise in the pulpit had not existed at all?

"Whether there be knowledge, it shall vanish away. For we know in part, and we prophesy in part; But when that which is perfect is come, then that which is in Fart shall be done away."

Oh God! What had he just said? His knuckles were white as he gripped the lectern harder.

"When I was a child, I spake as a child, I understood as a child, I thought as a child . . . "

As if in agreement the giggling had returned and this time it was coming from many of the pews below. Trilby's voice was coagulate and growing thin.

"But when I became a man, I put away childish things. For now we see through a dlass, garkly; but then face to face: now I know in *part*; but then shall I know even as also I am known."

Some below were now overcome by their mirth, choking it back under clamped hands and stuffed handkerchiefs. Other just silently quaked. Trilby had never tasted rage before and the bile of it was regurgitating into his mouth and spat out in the final words of the epistle onto the repulsive peasants below.

"And now abideth faith, hope, charity, these three; but the greatest of these *is* charity."

For once the organist's off-key blasts, throbs and whistles were welcome. It gave a pause for the canon to escape his tower of persecution and cover for other sounds to finally be fully released. The congregation stood and sallied forth into "Love Divine All Loves Excelling" and its uplifting cadence almost erased what had gone on before. It also masked the clatter of the late arrival of Wally Prince, the thrumming optimism of the hymn shaking his hangover and making him drop his cane. Only Chyme saw his arrival and quickly minced to the back of the church to reprimand his tardy interruption, his stiff heavy verge in his tight bird-like grip.

No one else was ever allowed to touch it and when it was not in use he had it locked away, or would take it home, letting all and sundry see his token of office. Wardens' staves, or rods as they are properly called, are generally kept upright at the end of special pews where they can be easily retrieved for more ceremonial occasions. But Verger Chyme's verge was quite a different matter. He had had it handmade in the finest ebony with a silver tip and a silver-plated steel cross adorning its head. It was four feet long and looked very much like any of the other ceremonial maces that gave the vergers their name and their right to bear arms in protection of their unarmed clergy. But Chyme's verge was not like the others because it was not solid all the way through. A two-foot sharpened steel blade slunk in the hollow part of its dark shaft. Cedric Chyme had been turned down by the enlisting officers of the Great War, when they were accepting anybody including pimple-faced urchins of the parish. Why they rejected him was never declared, but the disgrace of it haunted his wretched life and increased his sense of unyielding isolation. It also promoted a vengeful desire to become engaged in some species of physical violence, hence the invention of the sword-verge. And why not? He had met and seen many members of the aristocracy and gentry who carried sword-canes and sword-umbrellas, especially after the war.

The sight of the late and noisy stranger took the safety catch off of his brittle passivity and he took the verge in both hands, giving it the first twist to begin the unscrewing of the blade section. But as he approached closer, he saw the quality of the stranger's attire and sensed importance in his demeanour; recognised distinction in the cut of the man's jib. So by the time they came face-to-face Chyme had sheathed the fantasy of the blood-drenched dagger and was extending obsequious greetings to the abbey's new visitor. Both men instantly acknowledged a likeness in their stance in the world, a resonance in their higher callings. Chyme showed Prince to one of the rear pews and gave him the *Book of Common Prayer* and a hymnal. Prince nodded his appreciation and touched his lapel with two fingers. The verger was overcome with glee and made the appropriate response by slightly bending his arm across his chest. Both men knowingly smiled and separated, secure in the power of their secret order and its dominance over all things, even here.

Prince did not really care for the church. He tolerated priests because they could be useful and it was better to have them on your side rather than working against you. Normally, he would not bother showing his face at a service but in this affair of the ghost monk it seemed prudent. He had realised that he had got off on the wrong foot with Miss Garner. The maids in the inn had made that clear as he demanded "Just coffee and toast" while swearing under his breath and staring at his expensive wrist watch. He had to make a good impression on the dowdy hotel manager, because of her ties with the deplorable poet whose lilac-scented smugness reeked of benefaction. Prince suspected that the effete man was of the other persuasion, what back in New Cross they would have called a shirt-lifter or a nancy-boy. He himself had been called such in his youth—an insult that had nothing to do with his sexuality and was only ever attached to his solitary preference for books over loutishly kicking a ball about in the mud. Over the years he had proved his staunch masculinity with any number of attractive females, too numerous to mention. And even now as a Happily Married Man, he was often forced to beat off the attention of beautiful Fraus. His rich and elegant wife knew that she could trust him to save his virile and distinctive favours for her alone, at least when he was at home.

The hymn droned to a close and most of the singing ceased, except for one loud and discordant voice that continued at its own relentless pace. The organ and this horrible sound seemed to find a resonance with his empty stomach. He had forsaken a decent breakfast and rushed to be here this morning. The medicinal brandy, the half cup of bitter coffee, and the hastily nibbled toast sat ill at ease in his complaining innards. He clamped a hand over them and muttered under his breath. That's when he spotted the priest, the other reason why he was here—mixing with the multitude. He had done his homework and discovered that Montague Trilby was also a viscount in one of the most exceptional old families of the British Isles. A family known for their endowments to the arts and sciences. Although this was a meagre case, it was worth investigating because Trilby's connections made him a source of possible funding. Prince opened his prayer-book and stood up at exactly the same time as the rest of the congregation sat down. Chyme, who never took his eyes off him, winced tightly under his sombre alkaline face.

The prayers and lessons dragged on and the sermon was surprisingly stilted given the eminence of the man who delivered it. It was a concoction of Christian wisdom, scholarship deftly stirred into a bucketful of the "common touch", and obviously polished, but was weirdly delivered in a restless agitated manner, as if the good canon actually disliked his audience or the words he mouthed at them. The theme was the sight and insight, charity, and humility of the carpenter's son. It droned in and out of focus with the sleepy indifference of a nectar-drunk bumblebee.

During the section on the healing of Bartimaeus the Blind, Prince's eyes fell inward, sucking the heavy lids closed, though he did not feel it. Nor did he feel his huge jaw drop open. It was only the vociferous barking of his stomach that bolted him awake—awake to find the entire congregation staring at him. Even the priest had stopped in what looked like furious mid-sentence and was glaring down at him. Surely it was not that bad. How loud had it been? Surely such an experienced speaker would not be put off by a little innocent belly music? In total shock Prince made a few apologetic passes over his face with a fawning hand and an unpractised flurry of fingers over his waistcoated stomach, much in the manner of a moth that has discovered too late the fundamental nature of a naked flame.

Chyme had to do something to help his brother recover his dignity and jump-start the sermon again. He stepped one pace forward into the central isle and while all had their backs to him, he tapped three times with his heavy staff on the cold flagstone inscribed in the loving memory of Mary Juliette Agnew, Spinster of this Parish 1643-1701. It was a master-stroke. Everyone turned around and Trilby was jolted out of his contemplation of contempt and back into the compassion of Christ and the nobility of the act of giving. A good omen, Prince thought, if it had not been said through clenched teeth.

The actual Sacrament passed without incident. Notwithstanding, the canon still seemed watchful and suspicious of his flock as they approached and knelt at the altar rail. He fair glowered at Prince when he offered up his long bony hands to receive the host, the only sustenance he was likely to get before midday. His stomach was still growling, but it did so in a more demure manner and harmonised with the pre-lunch choir of the intestinal murmurs of the communicants kneeling in a row. After the service Prince decided to collar the canon and make a grovelling apology for his audible lack of breakfast. There must be some percentage in forsaking food for the benediction of the soul. On his way towards the miserable priest he passed the verger, and made another sequence of long-fingered signs and silent mouthings to explain his purpose. Chyme nodded sanction, and the ghost hunter nodded delight.

"Canon Trilby, please allow me to apologise for the errant noise I made before. Truth is I forewent breakfast in a rush to attend your fine service."

Trilby looked carefully at the overdressed man and smelt a rat. It might have been his sycophantic stance, or the over-familiarity of the man's lopsided smile. Prince's wet lips sliding over the long protruding teeth produced an uncomfortable displacement, like a slug in a button box. But most probably it was his accent. The clipped and inverted vowels had been over-cleaned and now possessed a rightness that was artificial and bleached of colour. Trilby knew this because he was also engaged in the same process, but in reverse. He was loosening his teeth and trying to swell his tongue into something that sounded faintly like the local parlance, in defiance of his upbringing and in a desperate need to join the broader mass of humanity. His experiences in Flanders during the last two years of that terrible war had made his need to shrink back from his birthright of power and dominion greater than his faith in God, and anything that prevented it or indeed reflected its hopelessness he saw as a malign influence and a personal attack.

Both men were standing on loose rungs of the ladder of the English class system, an eternal structure where every nuance of speech and behaviour declares a person's given status. But these two had defied the delineated height that had been allocated to them at birth, and were wilfully changing their ranks on the inflexible structure—Prince climbing up and Trilby climbing down. They were locked in an impasse where neither could see his own position, while being excruciatingly aware of the other's on the narrow vertiginous confine. Their awkward conversation outside the vestry was doomed from the start. Maudy Garner saw this out of the corner of her eye and misunderstood its meaning. Their body language and strained expressions showed that they separated into opposites—oil and water, chalk and cheese—which she read as good and evil. From the moment she had seen Prince for the first time she had known it. Then everything he did and said proved it. Her disappointment in the great man had curdled into dislike, distrust, and now a deep suspicion that he was very far from being a good man. This was *not* the person to be let loose on that poor lost spirit or were-man she had seen so badly used before. She edged her way out of the abbey, not wishing to catch his eye or anybody else's. She had a more pressing task to attend to.

"I am Walter Prince, founder of the Scientific Society for Psychical Research. You may have heard of it, or me?"

He was holding out one of his long manicured hands toward the canon who had no choice, being cornered, but to shake it. He expected a clammy, fish-like experience, but was surprised at the warmth and overt firmness of the grip.

Though Trilby betrayed no recognition, Prince pressed on.

"I am visiting your charming village at the request of one of your parishioners, a Miss Garner, to investigate the sighting of an apparition in your fine abbey. I do hope we might work together on this matter."

Prince already knew this man was going to prove difficult. His stiff and distant manner clearly signalled his disinterest, and something more. Prince had met a lot of people like Trilby: stuck-up snobs who preferred not to shake his hand and treated him with some disdain. He knew they were all intimidated by his ruthless quest for truth and overcome by the force of his personality. So he pressed on.

"I understand there have also been manifestations in the inn across the road, where I am currently staying. I would like to invite you for a drink there so we might discuss the matter further."

Chyme had suddenly appeared standing behind the insolent man, and the canon made frantic but disguised eye motions to him for help, salvation from this upstart. But the verger must have misunderstood because he sidled up beside Prince with a genial and unfamiliar smile.

"Prince, Walter Prince. A very good morning to you."

The men shook hands vigorously and Trilby was horrified to see a union between them.

"Cedric Chyme, the Verger of the Abbey."

"Yes, I know, I recognised your distinctive staff of office."

Chyme glowed and Trilby shivered.

"I was just explaining to Canon Trilby my purpose here in Pulborough and was seeking his advice in the matter. I am also certain your experience with the abbey will be of great value to my investigations."

Chyme, who had of course recognised the great man's name, swelled with pride and appeared to grow another few inches taller.

"I have seen it, seen it myself," he said.

"Really!" exclaimed Prince with the first signs of true interest. "Perhaps you would like to join me and your good canon here for a little libation in the Coach & Horses so that we might discuss the matter further?"

Chyme visibly recoiled like a snail sprinkled with salt, and the canon saw his chance of escape.

"I-I am afraid I don't imbibe," Chyme stammered. "I am a strict teetotaller."

The very idea made Prince cringe, though he did not show it, and, if only for a fleeting moment, the wind was taken out of his sails. Trilby stepped into the breach and dismissed himself before Prince could recover.

"Maybe another time. I am rather busy now and have a pressing appointment," he said.

And with that he had turned and was striding across the nave in a barely concealed canter.

Milky

Maudy was near the foot of the long sweeping bridge where the road divided into the main thoroughfare out of the village and the winding lane that led to the village outskirts, and suddenly beyond them to the open countryside. A great sense of elsewhere-ness haunted this periphery. It was more obvious in the evening, when streetlight dimming to ancient darkness marked the boundary. But even now in the windy cold approaching midday, a great difference could be perceived as Maudy turned into the side road—a muting of the hubbub of the rest of Pulborough. This corner of the world had the local name of Hob's Quarter, which referred to the low line of tumuli called Hob's Hollow that brooded just beyond the last village stile. Annabelle Chert's cottage was about halfway down the road at the bottom of a sharp turn under the bridge.

Maudy was surprised to find the garden gate unlatched, and looked towards the dull cottage windows. The wind was tearing at the trees and low bushes and rattling all that was not nailed down. She knocked on the door and waited. Then she knocked again, a sense of foreboding creeping upon her as she waited. She knocked again, and this time she thought she heard something that was not articulated by the wind. She stepped back and saw a face at the window. At first she did not recognise the gaunt blur as Mrs. Chert. Then the blur tapped and beckoned her close.

"Ars yourn bys yoursulf?" shouted the voice now behind the door.

"Yes, ma'am."

Screeching bolts were rustily pulled and the door snakingly opened, the old lady's eye peering through the crack. Then her thin arm lashed out and grabbed Maudy's and jolted her inside, where she stood in the freezing gloom as the bolts were rasped back again. The old woman looked wild and unkempt. For all her eccentric ways, Mrs. Chert had always kept some semblance of tidiness about her ragged persona. Not anymore—her hair was wild and uncombed, her eyes large and luminous and her multi-layered clothing without rhyme or reason.

"What ever's up, Mrs. Chert?" said the now alarmed Maudy.

" 'Im, dates wyats up. 'Im. His bin her everdid day. Outs theyre, a spyining ins ons mi."

"Who, Anna, who's been here?"

"That's wruungen, that's who."

Maudy hoped that she did not understand and decided to take control of the matter.

"Let me make you some tea," she said and guided the old lady towards the general direction of the kitchen, which had a modicum of warmth about it. Maudy sat Annabelle down in a chair and filled a large brown metal kettle, before discovering that the range was barely warm. And that the coal scuttle was totally empty.

" 'Tis freezing in here. You let the range go out?"

"Nosmore coal in 'ere."

"What about outside, in the coal house?

"I aints agyoin outs thar."

"But is there coal?"

"Aye, luts ofit."

"Then I will go and fetch some. It's freezing in here."

" 'Ims outs thar."

"No one's out there, I would have seen them."

" '*Ims* is."

"No, he ain't. I scared him off."

The old woman looked sideways at Maudy and saw that she was telling the truth. She was up out of her seat, the scuttle in one hand, a long metal key in the other.

"Be kwyks," she said, and pushed Maudy towards the back door.

The wind was stronger than ever and buffeted her towards the brick extension with the wooden door whose coat of green paint was shabby and peeling. She fumbled at the latch and let herself inside, adjusting her eyes and nose. Coal and logs sweetened and tarred the soft gloom as she nudged against forks, spades, hoes, and other sticks of wood that carried metal tool heads which mostly gave them function and appointment. They leant against the broken shelves that juggled old cans of paint, rusted tins of nails and screws, and many other things that had once been deemed useful. She picked up a short-haft shovel and was about to begin digging into the shallow pile of coal that had spewed across the flagstone floor, when she thought that she saw something in its midst that halted her. She strained her eyes into a tighter focus, squeezing the dominance of shadow back to the periphery. Then she moved from side to side to gauge her impressions of its shallow three-dimensionality. There, in the middle of the black sea, was an impression, a hollow as if a large dog or other animal had been nesting there. The twigs and loose dry leaves inside the circle were crushed and moulded into the shallow coal. She was wondering what manner of beast had been hiding there, what had let itself in and out by using the latch. Then she suddenly knew and a great shock overcame her. It was not fear, nor was it any form of alarm. It was an overwhelming wave of compassion, the like of which she had never felt before.

"It fair knocked me backwards," she would afterwards explain to herself and others. The potency of the blast made her drop the scuttle. She had always seen them, constantly around folk. Sometimes so real that it was difficult to tell the difference. But she had never understood their meaning or why their opacity and transparency varied so. But now, in this tiny brick hutch, the truth had been revealed and her heart had grown instantly through the wealth of it.

"*Yous ar cuminbyk?*" Annabel shouted, her face wedged in the crack between the door and its cringing frame.

The screech found its way into Maudy's other mind and reeled her back into the reality of the coal hole. She picked at the outer edge and filled the scuttle without disturbing the inner curved bed. Then she stumbled out into the wind again and into the face in the door.

"Fult youd gut lowst," the old woman said as Maudy emptied the scuttle onto the dying cinders of the straining fire. Maudy didn't respond, but raked the grate and opened the range's flue. The swirling wind above the thatched roof sucked deeply on the chimney until sparks and flames were snapped out of the reluctant embers.

"Didya spys 'im?"

"No, Anna. Ain't nobody out there."

A small quiet sat between them while the coal cracked and spat against the hollow wind.

" '*Im* bin therys ritanof, ate all my biryds grub 'im did."

Maudy said nothing.

"Evy skrawp orvit."

"Perhaps he needs it more than the birds," she said as the kettle began to splutter and hiss.

"*Nids it*, whadda fur? *Nids it. 'Im* don't havyve no rhyrts of enysfing. *'Im's* deed and surld be gworn. *Gwornouttovit.*"

Maudy ignored the old lady's furious agitation and retrieved the heavy steaming kettle to make the tea.

"Do you have any milk?"

"Cundenst," said Annabelle, pointing at the tin on the table. Maudy frowned at the tin and removed the two waxy plugs that had congealed over the ragged openings in the can of milk.

She reluctantly added it to the brew, where it formed a sullen and greasy undertow, but both women gained comfort from the tea's reassuring warmth.

After a while Maudy said,

"Do you like condensed milk, Anna?" distantly as if not expecting to hear an answer.

" 'Tisall I's got inahowse, taint bin owt, wid *'im* thar."

"Mmm."

"Whads wrung widit?"

"Nothing, just not the same, that's all."

"I's lyks it. Gut cuns ancuns of it udder theyr."

She pointed a bony finger at the Welsh dresser.

"Perhaps you should put some out," Maudy said wistfully, soaking up the growing dry heat and now seeming miles away.

"Owt?"

"Outside"

"*Puyt sum owytsyd?*"

"For the birds . . . Just for the birds."

Needy

After his post luncheon doze with the Sunday newspaper, Montague Trilby decided to have a bath to prepare him for evensong. He spoilt the water with a saturation of lavender crystals, which someone had once convinced him were both beneficial and elegant. He lay in the soothing grey-lilac water and tried to think of nothing, but every time he achieved it the giggle, the breaking of wind, and that horrid man's disgusting noises and odious presence jarred him back into annoyance. Who was this outsider who had wormed his way into Cedric Chyme's thorny confidence? Why were they both still jabbering about this ridiculous story of a ghost monk? It was just another exasperating irritation for him to deal with. There were so many these days and they seemed to be choking the thinking space between the nightmares of the past and his bright dreams of the future. He turned in the opaque water and felt a chill undertow pass beneath and to the side of him. He had been in the fluid for too long, his pale skin was beginning to become saturated. His last dregs of pigment dispersed somewhere within the enamelled white sarcophagus.

The abbey bells were ringing the evening in as Maudy trod the crisp ground back into the centre of the village. With the iridescent, painfully clear twilight came a drier cold than before. Not that she felt it. The rising stars in the brilliant air only qualified her belief in the wonder of all things. A great inner warmth tingled in every cell and shuddered with excitement beneath her plump layers of wool and cotton.

Even her breath, pluming before her or rising up to the heavens when she stopped to marvel at the night, demonstrated how an essence could be real and actual one minute and invisible and changed in the next. And how everything was knitted together in an almighty reverence, and that anyone with even half a heart could see it.

Mrs. Chert's words of anxiety and anger meant nothing to her. She had tried to explain to the old lady, but there was no use. She insisted on having it her way—seeing the presence of the monk as a "wrongun": a demented soul or demon that had come to haunt and persecute her for some unspecified sin she had committed in the past. Or even worse, a malevolent thing conjured up by a curse to cause injury, probably by those Pillocks. Hadn't the horrible thing been seen in their very pew?

This was the point at which Maudy had to leave the old lady. She had no intention of getting involved in slanderous gossip after her moment of revelation. As she walked she looked about, hoping to see the spirit so that she could declare her understanding and offer help and sympathy for its condition. But there was nothing on the frosty path, the main road, or the pavement. So she entered the back door of the Coach & Horses and made her way quietly to her little room, so that she could unbutton the wealth and expectations of her feeling there without getting them besmirched by William Penny or any such like.

One floor up and further over in what was called the east wing of the inn, Prince had uncorked a bottle of Scotch and was mumbling to himself about the rudeness of the toffee-nosed canon. He had started to make his famous casebook notes, but reached a blank after four sentences. There was very little to say at the moment. No evidence had come forth. He only had the statement of Verger Chyme, which he had carefully noted after a three-hour conversation over "Afternoon Tea", an English habit that he despised. This ghastly ritual had taken place in Chyme's cottage. He had insisted on it. Thank God Prince had had time to fortify himself with a half decent lunch and a few stiff chasers before attending at the given hour of 3:00 p.m. It was always 3:00 p.m. and it was always ghastly. Chyme had obviously been preparing the horror of it for hours, laying out his best china, butter knives, and finest teaspoons, all spotless and gleaming with self-righteous tea-totalism. Sandwiches and assorted cakes completed the landscape of chintz-ridden gloom.

Cakey

Chyme showed his brother into the cottage, pointing out the lowness of the beams almost in time. Then, after Prince had stopped rubbing his damaged Brylcreemed head and Chyme had stopped apologising they finally stooped into the tiny lace-infested parlour which he called the "drawing room". One look at the immaculate table confirmed Prince's worst suspicions. He was going to be here for hours. All sorts of delicacies had been prepared for him and each had a distinct and regimented place on the menu. His nervous eyes tried not to see the thin white bread sandwiches, their crusts amputated to encourage indecent anaemic curling, so that their interiors of sticky margarine and cold wet cucumber could be seen waiting for him. The cucumber had also been shorn of its delicate skin, the only part where flavour dared to reside. There were also finger rolls that dribbled a pink ichor, which he guessed was fish paste or canned salmon: the seemingly innocuous kind that always leaked water and concealed white spinal segments. Further up the English food chain and mounted on a silver and glass multi-tiered cake stand were the scones. Chyme pranced around the table, fussing with cutlery and napkins, and odious ornate holey rags that Prince thought were called doilies. His heart sank as he watched the verger behave so. Doubt or disapproval was never allowed between one brother and another. And he was desperately trying not to recognise that the man was a total wanker. Prince still kept

68

some of his former vocabulary to practise under his breath. Sometimes the vernacular precision could not be surpassed.

"Shall I be mother?" the verger said with a soupçon of femininity that made Prince clench his teeth behind the twitching hand that covered the lower half of his face. Prince nodded and half clucked while the huge teapot was being waved to and fro. Then he noticed a third cup waiting to be filled. Chyme caught his glance.

"Ah! Yes, Mother is joining us. I hope you don't mind, she is so looking forward to meeting you."

And then, like a cued entrance, she was suddenly there standing behind the famous and now startled visitor. She was small, ancient, and grinning. Dressed especially for him, he later learned. Dressed like a small child from a past century: a grubby Alice who looked like she was permanently in a Wonderland of her very own.

"Say hello to Mr. Prince, Mummy. He's the one I told you of."

She stepped into Prince's line of sight. Standing, she was no taller than he would be seated. She made a wobbling, sinking motion as if about to collapse. Prince was reminded of a dummy he had once caught a fake medium using. It was made of a dressed-up inner tube taken from some sort of large vehicle. It was pneumatically controlled by an accomplice using a hand pump in the next room. When it disappeared the air was simply let out, so that it could subside behind a convenient chair. Mrs. Chyme had exactly the same motion, which her son now seemed very proud of.

"That's a nice curtsy, Mummy. Now come and sit at the table."

She pulled her face into a rictus and moved her small hands tightly together and apart in a quick repeated action as if she playing a tiny concertina hidden in her lap. There was something shockingly lewd about the movement.

Then she instantly stopped and shuffled to the other side of the festooned table without taking her vacant watery eyes off Prince.

"Please join us," said Chyme to Prince, indicating a chair directly opposite the old lady. Prince sat down. Across from him only Mrs. Chyme's head showed above the lace table-cloth. At this proximity it became obvious she had randomly applied make up to her alarming face. Two circular spots had been daubed in the general area where her cheeks might once have existed. An eyebrow had been snakingly scrawled over her left eye. The other one had been forgotten or misplaced somewhere during the process. Then Prince saw her mouth. A smear of lipstick vaguely marked its approximate position. The irregularity might have been acceptable, but the colour was not. It was identical to the lurid hue that extruded from the sandwiches. Salmon pink, fish paste-rubicund, and of the same uneasy consistency. Prince looked away from the old woman's bloated stare.

"Please help yourself," insisted Chyme, who had positioned himself at some distance and was again waving the teapot.

"Are you pre- or post-lacteal?"

For one ghastly moment Prince thought that his host was asking this hideous question of his mother. Then he saw that it was directed at him.

"Milk first or after?"

Prince froze, trapped, knowing he had walked into a minefield of social interrogation. This meal above all others consisted of an array of invisible class snares. It was one of the reasons he so avoided it. Luncheon and dinner could be navigated and mastered. In his youth, during a weak moment of self despair, he had once considered becoming a butler and signed up on a short course. He had come to his senses on the fourth day after the true nature of the workload and its humiliating servitude had been revealed. But during that short time he had gleaned and collected all the devious contrivances and guile that masked a total lack of etiquette. He had improved those, beginning with a conscientious study of Larousse gastronomique and a scholastic memory of intimidating French wines. He now possessed the authority of a gourmet and the manners of a minor Baronet. He could grace, control, and manipulate any table in any hotel or home, no matter what lineage they fed from. But Afternoon Tea had been woefully bypassed in his anxiety to reach higher planes. He had no time for paltry repasts dominated by overbearing women and inconsequential men with nothing better to do than nibble and sip their way through lukewarm gossip for half the day.

"First then, we don't want to crack the bone."

What was this wretched man talking about? He was beginning to address Prince in the same way he did his senile mother.

"Pure bone china," piped Chyme, in a gleeful humour.

The tea was poured and various foods were insisted onto Prince's "bone china" plate. He ate what he could and drank some of the insipid tannin-brewed washing-up water. Why the English were so in love with this tea he would never understand. It must be the ritual, a version of the Chinese and Japanese ceremony, but perverted, with all the emphasis placed in the wrong directions. Apparently the previous discussion had been about the correct use of milk and its relationship with the cup, temperature and delicate nuances of homogeneous fusion. Fetishistic bunkum invented like so many other things such as napkin rings and sugar tongs to confuse and humiliate the lower class. He knew from his evening institute lessons in chemistry and physics that fluids met and exchanged in random molecular drift and that the order in which they were poured had nothing to do with it. This was a perfect model of the kind of thing that he had to deal with professionally every day of his working life, pitting his knowledge and experience against all sorts of ignorance and lies in his epic crusade against superstition and prejudice.

He had eaten two sandwiches and a finger roll. No sooner had his plate been cleared than it was laden again by the over-attentive Chyme. As the verger loaded the bone china with scones and cream he explained about his experience of the "monk".

"I have always had a sensitive nature. I got it from Mummy, who also saw many things when she was young."

Prince flicked a quick glance at the old woman, who was having some difficulty keeping the pastry in her mouth. She was using two of her stumpy bandaged fingers to tamp it deeply inside. Half of the fish-paste lipstick had vanished in the processes. Prince turned away, his own mouthful of scone heavy and dry.

"I don't think she has the gift any longer. Old age takes away many of our blessings."

He cocked his head on one side and relished her pathetic condition.

"She's not what she used to be, but is still useful about our home. Especially in the kitchen. She made the scones herself, you know."

The arid lump in Prince's mouth suddenly gained even more weight and shifted as if in surprise at hearing of its own generation.

"Her own recipe."

The old lady was now nodding ferociously and for the first time attempting speech. A spray of crumbs escaped in advance of the words, and her fingers, especially the injured ones, waggled as if to catch or net the errant food like so many diminutive panicked starlings.

"Called a murmuration," she said in a surprisingly deep voice.

Prince considered for a moment that she might be a tiny man dressed as a young girl in an old woman's skin, but the idea was far too grotesque, even for his standard. He had managed to swallow the sullen lump and was washing it down with the now stagnant tea, avoiding the hasty movements of her hands which were now stroking her chin in the manner of an ancient Chinese mandarin or sage. The notion of her mixing the dough with those hands was beyond contemplation.

"What is it, Mummsy?"

"Dems birds, dem starling birds," she said

"What you talking on—starlings? Why you talking about starlings?"

He turned and slid the conversation towards Prince.

"She sometimes goes off into a world of her own. You must forgive her, she is very old now."

"Of course, of course," said Prince. "But she is right, a murmuration is the collective noun for a flight of starlings."

And as he said the name of the bird, the penny dropped and turned the cogs that exposed the meaning of all the previous quick shuffling, chin stroking and cranium tapping that her mobile hands had performed before. He was astonished and looked more closely at her, which brought her great merriment.

"Now, now, Mother. Best behaviour please."

"My God, she is psychic," Prince exclaimed, and Chyme stopped scolding his mother and frowned at his guest's blasphemy.

The shuffling had been her mime for a hand pump as he was thinking it and the rubber tyre dummy. The chin stroking was a sign for a man. The cranium tapping meant cleverness, as in "now you understand". And the conversation about the collective name for starlings was instigated by his passing image during her flurry of crumbs. She had seen all the thoughts instantaneously, at the very moment they had appeared in the ghost hunter's mind, and then responded with great accuracy and humour.

"She has her ways," Chyme answered cautiously.

"It's astonishing."

"It's just her way."

"Truly extraordinary."

"Yes, yes, but I was telling you about the monk. What I have seen and also what I have heard from others."

The old lady was now making a pinching gesture with her left hand and thumb, much like that of a bird, indicating that her son was talking too much. Prince smiled and the verger saw it.

"Are you no longer interested in my testimony?" he said sharply.

"Yes, of course, but I was overwhelmed by your mother's abilities. I was—"

"Then I shall continue," cut in Chyme. "Do you have a notebook? My account is rather detailed."

The old woman was just about to make another comment when her son snapped at her, "It's time for your nap."

There was no arguing with him. She was dismissed as quickly as she had arrived, shuffling across the room while her son spitefully buttered another parched scone.

Almost two hours later Prince fled the cottage; he had not seen Mrs. Chyme again. His request to say goodbye was flatly turned down. He knew that she was awake and aware somewhere about the tiny cottage, and thought that he could feel her probing his mind as he was rushed through the corridor and onto the sleeting street. It was such a wasted opportunity; she would have made a brilliant case study.

He had enough portable equipment with him to test her thoroughly. He knew his chances of getting her to London were negligible, but thought that he would be able to charm or cajole the irritating verger into at least a limited session. In this, like so many other things, he was woefully wrong. But now he had more pressing business. He turned his coat collar up and bent into the wind, gaining speed against it until he reached the door of the inn and the redemptive fug of the warm bar.

Karsi

The next few days saw an increase in the general interest in the "Ain't There Monk" as it was beginning to become known. More strangers were arriving in Pulborough, and were seen vacantly hovering about the street and the abbey grounds. Business at the Coach & Horses was brisk and sometimes even crowded. Many had come when they heard that the "Ghost-Finder General" himself was staying in the village and carrying out experiments in the presence of the general public. Prince didn't much care for the name that the London rags had mutually found for him. He had a much better one himself. The "Ghost-Finder General" sarcastically alluded to the fact that he had never arisen above the rank of corporal in the Great War. And more unpleasantly aligned him to the infamous Mathew Hopkins, the Witchfinder General who had been given the title in the 1640s by King Charles I and Parliament. Over a fourteen-month crusade he tortured and executed hundreds of women to scourge England of the malign presence of witches. Such a moniker would have hurt and humiliated a lesser man, but Prince had the hide of a rhino and the ego of Wellington. Secretly he even thought that they shared the same distinctive profile, so that such a meagre slight was easy to disregard. Nevertheless, it did give him notoriety, which drew in the crowds.

"A confounded nuisance," he would say in public. "An unfortunate crowd getting in the way of serious scientific investigation."

He was always mild in his scathing—it would not do to alienate their curiosity or to force their hand in branding him a hypocrite or a mountebank. After all, it had been his enquiries to the local press via the stolid Miss Wainscoot in London that had told all and sundry that he was on a secret investigation somewhere in the home counties. Further details about the case, that it concerned a local spinster woman and the abbey, were added later, when the initial kindling had not fully ignited.

All sorts of people came into the bar of the Coach & Horses, seeking out the Ghost-Finder. Some of the more affluent looking actually found him, and, after insisting on buying his lunch or dinner and any number of Uncle Billy's best single malts, they might be "let in" on his latest findings and speculations about the case.

Other strangers watched at a distance the peculiar antics of some of the locals. They watched Cedric Chyme continually creeping around every corner and recess of the abbey building and examining every inch of the churchyard, probing its boundaries, undergrowth, and shadows with his formidable staff of office. They may have even seen old Mrs. Chert in some of the brighter daylight hours scurrying around the outskirts of the village, looking very carefully at the slowly increasing layers of snow. The most observant could possibly have seen Maudy Garner's sideways glances and the little flutters of her eyes in and about the general area and influence of the Coach & Horses. For she had taken to spending odd moments of her busy day in the back yard, or where the old stables used to be, or outside on the street between the abbey lych gate and the arch of the old coaching yard. She would have said that she engaged with the inn's business, and nothing else, but the most critical observer would have noticed that her attention was not fully devoted to the chores in hand, and a sliver of her sight was always sideways, checking the peripheries around her with a care that was far beyond the casual.

Even the canon himself had taken on an austere, reserved inspection of his domain, to ascertain if any of these quaint rumours had grounding in fact. As he strode through the chancel he peered down the quadrant of his long nose in the general perspective of the Pillock pew, and of course saw nothing other than a shifting blur. He snatched off his spectacles and wiped them on the edge of his surplice. When he returned them to his squinting sight, nothing out of the ordinary remained in the clarity of his vision.

"There has been an infinity of spectres reported over the centuries. All kinds and species of apparitions have been reported by the most learned and trustworthy observers. It would be foolish to dismiss all of these as works of the imagination or optical illusions. For my part I like to keep an open mind and bring a scientific understanding to all reported phenomena. That is what makes my studies so unique. Indeed, it is my quest to bring a fresh objectivity to this twice-told tale."

This was not the first time that Wally Prince had made this speech. It was the preamble to his declaration of personal genius, which generally worked if it had only been heard once or twice before. But this was the fourteenth time that Uncle Bill had heard it and he had no intention of listening to it again, so he slid his vast size backwards away from the table of gawping strangers who surrounded Prince, and squeezed it sideways through the back door into the corridor under the stairs. He would not normally have tolerated having such a gobshite permanently entrenched in his bar. But this one was bringing in the trade, and some part of the landlord's skinny tolerance marvelled at the sheer audacity of the man.

Billy pushed himself out to the gents in the yard, not having the energy or the inclination to climb the three flights of stairs up to his own private toilet, which still contained some signs and leftovers of his departed wife: bits of chintz and chinoiserie which he hadn't the heart, or the energy, given his total indifference, to expel.

The out-building had a tiny oil stove in it, the kind used by some poultry farmers to stop their hens from freezing to their eggs. Billy had not put it out there for the sake of his patrons, but to prevent the pipes and cold water tank from seizing up. But in the depth of this weather it made no impression on the thick snow-covered roof and the icicles that spiked down from the guttering. The squat brick structure was cold and empty—exactly the way he liked it. There was something about its hissing pipes, deep harsh scent of disinfectant, and tang of paraffin that satisfied Billy. There were no frills about it and its constant masculine chill kept women away. He pulled out his old jack knife, selected the right blade and inserted it with great skill and practice into the inner lip of the bulky brass lock that demanded a penny to gain access. He had no intention of ever spending any of his hard-earned money on natural functions. Even if the valuable coin would eventually find its way back into his own pocket. It was a matter of principle. Some rituals just have to be obeyed, no matter what the circumstances.

The lock gave up the ghost with a resentful cluck and he snuggled into the tight space and unbuttoned, de-belted, and de-braced himself before enjoying the hardness of the freezing seat. He shuffled about, making himself comfortable on the complaining wood and then took out his flaccid ancient pouch. In between the extended ruminating time of pipe smoking, Billy rolled cigarettes (or rather, baggily folded them using the same thick tobacco). The karsi was no place for pipe smoking; it took too long, needed both hands, and seemed in some way unsanitary. But a cigarette had decency about its duration and the smoke was another warning of his belligerent occupation.

He lit up the scruffy cigarette and began quietly pondering about the problems and joys in his daily life. He must have been there about five minutes before somebody else entered the out-building. He had been speculating about spending the extra cash he had made that month, and how he might use it during the next market days in Great Tidings. Certain ladies came into the county's market town at that time, and he would be able to purchase some of their more exotic delights; something which he did not object to spending "a few bob" on. He was picturing his mastery over one of the younger Irish girls when his reverie was instantly broken by the intrusion outside. He even muttered a curse under his steaming breath. The other person who now shared the karsi was very quiet and did not appear to be making the normal sounds of unbuttoning, sighing, and coughing that are so important to the satisfactory observance of good masculine urinary behaviour. In fact, it was quieter out there now than it was before. The lead pipes seemed to be less vocal, as if the water itself was also listening, and the crows and wind outside had abated. Billy wondered if the other man had changed his mind and left as quietly as he had entered. Then the noise of the coin-operated latch on the next cubicle dented the air and notched a jagged shock into his heart. It all went silent again. No sounds of undressing or sitting down, and even more alarming—no sounds of the cubicle's door being shut and locked. What kind of man would behave like that? Billy drew himself away from the wooden panelling of the connecting wall and accidently rubbed heavily against the small wooden shelf holding the square box of Izall toilet paper, knocking it askance and sending a cascade of the brittle sheets scurrying to the floor. For a moment, the horror of such a waste distracted his unease. It was *her* fault, *she* had insisted on removing the traditional bits of newspaper on a string and replacing them with this expensive razor-sharp slippery stuff. What business did she have poking about in the gents anyway? *She* said it was not proper for the better kind of customers they were getting now. It was "bad enough that the real gents had to go outside, let alone be affronted by dingy scraps of old newspapers". He had pointed out that it was *The Times* (the only rag that he ever read). *She* said it made no difference, and he eventually gave in, the idea of the expense of interior plumbing allowing *her* to think that she had won the battle.

Billy clutched at the falling paper as if it had been Maudy's throat. Then someone giggled, a very very small rhythmic titter that was not the pipes. A response to his ridiculous predicament. Something was laughing at him. He let go of the mangled paper and swivelled around to face the wall, ready to bellow abuse. Then the mouthful of scolding words began to turn soar and soapy as the oddness of the situation took hold. Another man was out there, just beyond the panelled partition, giggling. Giggling in the gents was something that no proper man would ever be caught doing. What kind of pervert would do that? Maybe it was a passing lunatic, or worse—a queer. Or both. He suddenly felt exposed and vulnerable and shrank in the cold of it. He pulled his trousers about him, but was not able to cover the vast expanse of his belly without standing and further proclaiming his predicament. Then those dreadful feelings became worse, because a sense of the uncanny crept in to join the abnormal. *Come on, pull yourself together*, he told himself. All those old wives' tales were infecting him, and the twaddle that Prince was spouting. At this rate he would be worse than Maudy Garner with all her ghosts and ghoulies. He tried to shake off the dread that was overcoming him but the silence outside was worse than ever, which made every noise he made twice as loud. Whoever was out there was now listening to him. The eeriness of that made his flesh creep, and the cigarette fell out of his now-uncertain hand. He did not know whether to bellow, yank up his trousers, and kick the door open to confront the person in the next cubicle, or to keep still and hope for them to go away. Fear had entered his booth and he shut his eyes tight for a second, as if to squeeze the horror away.

A hiss made him blink them open—a hiss close enough to be in the cramped chamber with him. It came from below and he cast his shivering eyes down to the floor. The hiss came from his dropped cigarette. It hissed because a pool of water, or some other liquid, was flowing in from under the door. No, not the door but the gap at the bottom of the partition to the cubicle next door. It was in there next to him. Billy let out a strangled cry and sprang from his seat, one hand grabbing at his trousers, the other fumbling the lock. He stumbled out with his braces snapped off in his hand, his belt hanging like a vacant tail and his trousers and voluminous underpants totally fallen and wrapped tightly around his shuffling shoes. The liquid had been absorbed into their thick tweed and the thin cotton, and he felt something of its damp against his bare white ankles. He tried to run, but each movement only tangled him more until his feet stopped dead and his immense weight toppled forward. He fell heavily and lay winded, whimpering, and waiting for the door of the other cubicle to open behind him.

Injury

To his astonishment the canon had found something a little less than ordinary under the spiral stairs that corkscrewed up to the clock tower and belfry. It appeared to be some kind of nest made of cassocks and hymn books. The latter had been turned inside out, broken back against their spines so that their paper innards were turned upwards to make an array of squashed ruffs. But strangest of all, one of the spare brass altar crosses had been laid at its centre in what looked like some kind of ritualistic manner. Such manifestations of bizarre totem offering rubbed against every fibre of Trilby's upbringing and beliefs; he found such oddities offensive and distasteful.

He had been tiptoeing around the installation when he heard a noise from above: a slight clatter on the steps, metallic and hollow. It appeared to be descending. He stood erect, flattened against the blind wall beneath the stairs. An equal degree of stealth was being practised by whoever was coming down. Trilby had not felt anxiety until he saw the glimmer of steel. A long thin blade appeared in advance of the feet of its owner. Trilby's blood ran cold; he had seen what a bayonet could do. And the dammed-up memories of its atrocities flooded back. Suddenly he was overcome by the instinct of fight or flight, and it took possession of his actions. He slid forward and snatched up the heavy brass cross from the nest and swung it hard like a weighty scimitar at the now visible knees of the blade-carrying intruder. A ragged scream rang out;

echoes of it ran up the tower to lick at the frosted interior of the great iron bells before cascading down the spiral stair and taking the long spear-like weapon with it. Trilby moved sideways as it clattered against the stone, and was ready to swing the cross again into the falling sobbing man when he recognised the other end of the weapon. Its ornate silver-plated cross instantly made itself known as Cedric Chyme's verge. He stepped back as the verger fell after it in ungainly wincing agony.

The slicing blow of the brass crucifix had split Chyme's kneecap and dislodged a mass of connective tissue beneath. In his youth, Canon Trilby had been a demon batsman for his varsity cricket team and had enjoyed being part of the village side. Although horrified about the damage he had inflicted on the poor verger, some small part of him was proud that he had not lost his savage touch. He extracted the broken man from the staircase and helped him hop across the room to the nest of cassocks and books, where he collapsed.

As Chyme thrashed around clasping his leg, Trilby vaguely remembered something from his time with the Classics. Wasn't it the ancient Greeks who believed that a man's vitality, his power, resided in his knees? And that semen was manufactured there? There was certainly a great deal of leakage around poor Cedric's distended joint.

"I will get you a medic, Cedric. Just hold on."

The verger swore viciously under his pain and shot dagger glances at the canon.

"I'm very sorry, but I did not know it was you. I just saw the weapon and heard you creeping about."

Chyme swore again and grated his teeth.

"After all, how was I to know that you had such a fearsome thing?"

He had picked up the gleaming "business end" of the verge and was examining its rather poor workmanship. He then probed about with its point among the nest.

"Did you make this?

"Course not," grimaced Chyme. "I just put the cross on it to keep the monster off."

"What monster?"

"The bloody monk. He made it, he's been hiding in here."

"For how long?" asked the astonished Trilby.

"I don't know," said the wincing verger. "I have always found odd things like this in and around the abbey, but I put them down to kids or vandals, not this."

Trilby looked at the wounded man for signs of shock or delirium. Chyme saw the look and it fired his rage.

"I am not mad, I know what I am talking about. There's been a 'nest' here for years, especially out there in the churchyard. I thought it was muntjacs."

He paused to take a painful breath between clenched teeth.

"But now I know different, now he's come inside. *Well, I won't have it.* Not in here, it can find somewhere else to make its nest. I am not having a tramp, or a stinking monk, or *whatever* infesting my abbey. If you won't drive it out then I will."

That night the canon had a restless and disturbing time. He could not sleep for fear of waking and could not wake for fear of sleeping. So in between those illusionary states whose very edges are abraded by all the uncertainties of reality, he rose and fell and sought anything for consolation. Even a fiction of guilt he had never possessed. Surely it was the grievous injury he had inflicted on his verger that distressed him so. What else could it be? It must be that, perplexing his rest. Yet he had seen so many things in the trenches and the splintered oozing land between them that nothing could unstring him now, and certainly not the hiding places of a vagrant man masquerading as a monk. No, it could not be that. He rolled over again, pulling the sheet and blankets with him and curled up inside their rumpled protection. Just before dawn he fell deeply into waking where he dreamt of the nest of books and kneelers, their substance and purpose exchanged so that the words were spongy, knotted and sewn and the cushions were ruffled or tight, silent and closed.

Bacony

"Maybe something happened when Bill laid hands on him?" said Jenny absently. "Him being the only one to ever touch it and all."

Maudy suddenly saw the wisdom in the young woman's words.

"How do you mean?" she asked.

"Don't know really. But Bill had no doubt about him, and p'raps some of it rubbed off, like."

"What, made him believe in 'imself?"

"Kind of, but in another kind of way. More real, like."

The girls looked at each other across the sizzling kitchen, the rolling smell of breakfast more dominant than the morning light.

"Made tangible," said Maudy, as if she were tasting a different air.

And as she thought, there, in its clarity, the rich smell of bacon scrolled its way out of the room of women and entwined and insisted itself into every corner of the inn. In the empty bars it strangled out the sullen aroma of stale beer and tobacco and rose up to penetrate the plaster ceiling. On the carpeted stairs it crept up to illuminate every landing. Doors and floorboards could not hush its flow, and as it ascended it found the noses of the pale pyjamaed men, exotic in their hangovers and fears.

Along the twisting corridors of the first floor Walter Hugh Prince was distressed by the morning's arrival. Those that had come to pay court all day yesterday had insisted on buying him drinks. Even when he attempted to staunch the continual flow they would not listen or did not hear his modest denials, given in a soft-spoken tone so as not to insult their generosity. He had been talking for hours, wasting his valuable research time, and when the hungry masses left him he felt overtired and drained by all the knowledge he had imparted. But such is the way of the scientific pioneer, determined on bringing such a shy subject into the rude glare of public opinion. Why should the universal truth be kept solely for the academics? What right did those pompous snobs have to hog all the wisdom and keep it imprisoned for themselves? No, no, it was the man-on-the-street who understood his campaign and supported his rise to the well-earned status of absolute expert. That is why they were so keen to gather and plaudit him, and show their affirmation by purchasing far too many libations to toast his unique position. The excitement of it all made his head ache even more, so that when the salty greased tongue of bacon slid under his door it made his stomach dance in a convulsion that was not measured in merriment or appetite.

One floor up in the private rooms at the top of the inn, William Penny had not left his bed, his twitching red-rimmed eyes glaring at the locked door. The sheets and blankets covering his vast bulk made his shape indecipherable. Only his poor pink head sticking out of the mass declared his humanity. He had sworn abstinence since his ordeal in the pub's outhouse, and now the effects of shock and withdrawal were taking their toll. Bits of his bedroom were taking on a malign and animated nature; certain mischievous and disrespectful socks were nudging each other while whispering and scurrying to and fro beneath the armchair that he had always used (and trusted) before to contain his nightly sheddings. Now it too had taken on unnatural tendencies, groaning and shifting its stance in what appeared to be annoyance or lewd posturing in the periphery of his blurred vision. It flexed its creaking inner anatomy of dusty horsehair, fatigued springs, and sagging strapping in an ungodly and suggestive way. He could even hear its hoary leather skin complaining as its weight shifted awkwardly on its carved bowed legs, as it responded to the waft of bacon that had just picked the lock.

Statuey

Outside the weather had turned cruel, making the high street and churchyard no place for man nor beast, nor anything else. Smelling the frost and hearing the moaning wind, many shivered in the post dawn and pulled their blankets and partners closer about them, deciding that bed was the best place to be and the rest of the day was best left to others.

Only one figure could be seen abroad. It was up near the Hob's Quarter where the wind had hold of an unlatched door and was ferociously banging it towards a point of distress that it would never recover from. The sound of it was caught under the white curve of the great stone bridge, where its reverberations were elongated into an eerie resonance that gathered velocity towards the heart of the village. It could now be heard in the subconscious interiors of most of the shuttered houses, even behind the thickest curtains and under the loudest snoring.

Eventually somebody said, "What's that banging?"

An hour or three later, when the sun lied about its warmth and the wind lost some of its spite, the knocking became less urgent and almost rhythmic. Thomas Yates pulled on his chilled Wellington boots and heavy overcoat and forced his way out into the day. He had his cap pulled down and his scarf pulled up to keep the cold off his face, giving him a visor slit of sight into the white world, which was beginning to give him some pleasure with its bright purity.

As he approached the Quarter he saw the snowman close to one of the buttresses of the bridge. It had been made to be framed by the great arch above it and appeared slightly stooped, as if influenced by the mighty stone. A small ragged end of scarf fluttered near where its neck should be. The rest was smothered beneath impacted surface layers. Yates smiled under his own scarf as he traipsed towards it, appreciating the detail its maker had put into creating such a realistic effect. He grinned foolishly when he saw the pair of spectacles imbedded in the snowman's head, and was just about to laugh at the staring pebbles for eyes when he recognised the snowman as Mrs. Annabelle Chert.

Alice stood in the kitchen wringing her apron in her bony blue, knuckled hands. She had just told Maudy about the horrible find and was sharing, or pretending to share, her shock and twitching grief. After another five silent minutes, Maudy turned and headed towards the street.

A small group of people stood around the ambulance, whose purring engine was melting a black shadow into the white road beneath it. The pillar of snow had only just been prised out of the vertical and now lay crushing the waiting stretcher with a grimly comic horizontality. It had slid and toppled out of the embrace of the two uniformed men who were still frozen in their gestures of loss, their arms outstretched and confused like somnambulists. Three villagers gawped on, their jaws and eyes locked open in disbelief.

"Don't just leave her lying there," puffed Maudy as she trotted into the tableau.

The taller of the two ambulance men found some words in his flapping mouth.

"She fell over," he said convincingly.

Thomas Yates explained to Maudy that it was he who had found her so, and had called the ambulance from the rectory. He gave a detailed account of his heroic attempts to revive the statuesque figure of Mrs. Chert, and explained that he had only given up when her nose came off in his hand.

"Sounded like a bit of celery, it did."

Meanwhile the uniformed men were wrestling with the prone white figure, attempting to break off the frozen casing so that she might fit into the collapsed stretcher. But the icy wind had deeply compacted the layers of snow. The last solid remains of poor Annabelle just skidded back and forth, with only her Wellington boots escaping the encapsulation and sticking out of the end of her statuary at a strange and immodest angle.

"Better get a kettle, Ted," said the smaller kneeling man.

"Take more than one," said the taller one, now identified as Ted.

"You could lean her up agin' the exhaust pipe," said Old Darius Munt, who had emerged from his long caped coat and deerstalker hat much in the same way as a suddenly ravenous tortoise does after hibernation.

He was obviously enjoying himself, and of course did not hear Maudy's horrified exclamation at his improper suggestion.

"Prop her under the tailboard," he insisted, his head making small darting actions back and forth to emphasise his point.

The ambulance men were confused by his commanding upper-class tone and took their gloved hands off of Mrs. Chert while they considered his idea.

"*Don't you dare*," demanded Maudy.

The force of her command must have dislodged something in the broken stretcher, because the bottom rung of it suddenly came adrift and the prone ice edifice of Mrs. Chert slid forward, gaining rapid momentum on the now slippery ground. She trundled feet first, away from the startled men and swiftly disappeared under the ambulance where she came to rest in the dark thawed puddle.

"*Don't just stand there*," shouted the now distraught Maudy as she moved forward to give instructions to the growing crowd.

The problem was that now the body was so far under the vehicle that nobody could reach it, and a quiet unspoken dread prevented any of those present from crawling beneath to grasp it. No one thought of moving the ambulance. Or if they did, they kept it to themselves. Probably because of fear of a further unspeakable sacrilegious accident.

Eventually Thomas Yates found a solution and improvised part of the broken stretcher into a hooked pole, much like those used by anglers to land heavy and struggling fish. He got on his knees and probed about blindly under the ambulance, trying to gain some kind of purchase. After much panting and muttering he finally made a substantial contact and heaved on the pole, slowly pulling the figure into the group of bystanders who now numbered over a dozen. Most of them shrank back when she slid, (again on the unthawed snow) rather rapidly into their presence, almost knocking Darius Munt asunder.

It was the manner of the random fastening which caused the consternation and repulsed alarm. The bent piece of steel at the far end of Yates' improvised gaff had hooked through the shattered spectacles of the old lady, and she had been dragged out by their bent wire that was twisted through her frozen and nose-less face. Yates dropped the pole, and its icy clatter was the only sound until Maudy quietly said,

"Just get a blanket and get her inside the van."

Ted stared at her in shock.

"*Van?*" he said, finally galvanised into action by the outrage of the woman's slight against the majesty of their ambulance.

Back at the Coach & Horses, Prince had fortified himself and decided it was time to grasp the bull by the horns, or rather the canon by the enigma. He stepped into the cold air with a shiver and a determination to find the spiritual significance of the tramp in the pew.

Montague Trilby was in the abbey praying in the quiet of the Lady Chapel. He did not often pray in public sight, preferring contemplation and reflection in the silence of his study. The enclosure of books worked as a tensile baffle that accumulated his meditation and encouraged the divinities and powers to listen and judge his dedication.

After the ambulance had gone and the crowd had dispersed, Maudy stood alone, staring at the isolated black water shadow of revealed road. The wind had faded and only drew attention to itself by the flurries of snow it whisked out of the trees and off rooftops, and the now limp banging of the distant door. She turned and headed back towards the centre of the village, and away from the arches of the bridge. As she walked, the banging identified a possible source. She stopped, then she knew where it was coming from.

Mrs. Chert's garden was dazzlingly white. The trees and bushes were gleaming as if made of glass, and everything seemed to be opening to communicate more deeply with the last moment of winter. It was not what she had expected. Even the spasms of the wrecked front door seemed muted by the tingling atmosphere. She moved into the enclosed space and let its impossible influence calm her. As she put her hand on the door to still its anguish, it instantly let go of the wind and slumped back into reluctant closure. She half considered stepping inside, intending to call out, ask if anybody was there. Then she changed her mind and firmly pushed against the cold wood, turning the knob in the splintered hasp to make sure that it stayed closed. She did not inspect the out-building because she already knew that the depression in the leaves and coal would be gone. There was nothing here anymore; "it" had no purpose in being here. She left the illuminated garden, wistfully touching the crystal ice and its leaping glow. Outside the gate the world seemed duller, but respectful. The wind had gone and the way back to the inn felt short and untroubled. Even the shallow impressions of sandaled feet before her seemed ordained, natural, and benign.

Stuttery

The Ghost-Finder General cleared his throat at the back of the Lady Chapel, and it was heard by the canon at the edge of supplication. Prince did it out of nerves and smoking, he always had. It matched his twitches and ticks and the constant adjustments of cuffs, tie, and pipe. It also sometimes came in useful to announce his important presence, but was without wilful artifice. It was one of his only characteristics that he could not use consciously; like stuttering, it could not be manufactured for effect. The years of schoolroom torture could not be inverted and puppeted.

"Canon Trilby, when you have a moment I would like to talk."

He took a quiet pew at the front of the chancel.

Three-and-a-half minutes later Trilby gritted his teeth, stood up and slowly moved towards Prince. Prince rose as the tall stooping figure loomed over him.

"Thank you, Canon, for accepting my invitation."

Trilby had no idea what he was talking about.

Prince motioned to a position beside him on the pew as if he owned it.

"How did it happen?" asked Jenny as she and Alice stood in the warm kitchen and watched the pale, seated figure of Maudy sip her tea.

"She got caught in the freeze, out there, under the bridge."

Maudy's voice was far off, but not distant and nowhere near the freezing bridge.

"But why?" insisted Jenny.

"She was searching out there, looking for signs."

Jenny did not understand and looked over Maudy's head to Alice on the other side of the table. She silently mouthed the word "signs" at her, hoping for an answer. Alice shook her head and puckered her mouth to tell the girl to leave the matter alone. Alice had seen Maudy arrive back at the inn, saw her looking at the snow-covered ground, and its whiteness reflected in her unstrung gaze. Saw her pause next to the old coach and rest her hand on the handle of its permanently sealed door.

"Poor ol' soul didn't understand it at all," continued Maudy.

Then she looked up out of her reverie, straight into the eyes of the confused Jenny.

"You got it right, girl. Knows how it all works."

Jenny was about to confess total ignorance when Maudy said, "Out of the mouths of babes and angels."

"The truth is I have had quite enough of your village's folk tales, and now every Tom, Dick, and Harry wants me to explain the phenomena to them. I thought it was about time to have a sensible discussion with somebody who might add a bit of depth and dimension to what's going on here," said Prince, twisting his neck in an uncomfortable rigor.

"I really don't think I can help you in any way," said Canon Trilby curtly.

"Oh, come now! We are both men of insight. I promise no harm will come to your reputation or the good standing of the abbey. I simply want your view on this event," said Prince.

"This 'event' seems to have gotten completely out of hand and 'my view' on it is to ignore it and get on with the daily business of the church and the administrations of God's benefaction."

"But surely you have heard all the evidence, and believe some kind of spiritual phenomena have occurred here?"

"I have heard a lot of rumours and some near hysterical suppositions from the more eccentric of my parishioners."

"I would hardly call Verger Chyme hysterical," stabbed Prince.

"That's a different matter. My verger is a man of great integrity and—"

"You believe him then," interrupted Prince.

"It's not about what I care to believe."

"Oh, but it is."

"I simply don't see the point in all this. Such matters are best left undisturbed."

"And swept under the carpet?"

Prince's blood was beginning to rise, and he was relishing his upper hand and the canon's back foot.

"The business of the church is to focus spiritual matters into a common good and share in the depth of the non-material world."

"You make it sound like communism."

"I most certainly do not," spluttered Trilby. "What right have you to question me?"

"I am undertaking a serious investigation into psychic phenomena."

"What, from the taproom of the Coach & Horses?" scoffed Trilby, and it put Prince's confrontation out of gear.

He flinched and rallied forth.

"M-my investigations in that quarter were a s-series of interlocking interv-v-views . . . "

The canon heard the concealed stutter and understood what it meant.

"The conversation of drunks has no interest for me, my training precludes such nonsense when investigating the complexities of other dimensions of being."

Prince's face began to twitch and his hands began to curl and dither under the priest's attack. Trilby saw this and pushed home.

"The rigour of an academic education teaches one how and when to apply certain philosophical rules and measures that naturally eliminate all the rubbish that you listen to, collect, and believe. The Classics teach wisdom on a profound level and a seminary training gives the knowledge of application, if you see what I mean."

Prince saw it all right, and none of the usual slippery arsenal of his rhetoric could parry the canon's painful assault. He stuttered and blenched, his teeth nagging his lower lip while he waited for the right words to fight back.

"The point is, old chap, is that it does not matter what you think, and anything I have to say would just add to your stockpile of irrelevance. No matter how blatant the evidence, it all becomes invalid inside your method of investigation. Therefore it's a total waste of my time."

"B-b-but—"

"No b-b-buts about it."

And here Trilby made the fatal error of parodying Prince's stutter, a crime that is never left unpunished. The stutterer can and must endure all manner of disrespect, misunderstanding, and smirking abuse, but the sarcastic imitation of his or her stutter is quite simply unforgivable, and places its perpetrator inside the inner ring of vindictive revenge. Something inside Prince turned icy and began to be sharpened, some of the sparks of this process accidentally illuminating a word that the canon had let slip.

Prince retracted his teeth, took a deep breath and said it: "Blatant."

"Who is?" said the canon.

"You said blatant."

"W-what?" Now it was Trilby's turn to stumble over his words.

"Blatant, you said there was blatant evidence. What have you seen that was so blatant?"

"No, I meant to say . . . "

And he did not know what he meant to say. His practised varsity debating skills drained away as he confronted the image of the nest of books and cassocks. He was suddenly beached there among them, high and dry with only the limping verger as Man Friday, or worse—a vindictive witness.

"What was it that you saw, Canon?"

Invisibility

Eight pews behind them, something was watching the back of their heads and darting to and fro. It mumbled to itself as the two men continued to squabble over its existence and their own place in this lopsided world, where all things were slippery and continually shifting their purchase and meaning.

The lofty shadows on the pale ceiling began to throb and exchange shape as the voice of the great organ opened into the abbey. It was a practice morning and normally only the organ master would be there. He did not even notice the combatants in the front pew, and they merely raised their voices and leant into each other's space to continue their dispute. The overlapping eddies of sound embraced the architecture and swelled the different volumes of light in a vast, timeless concord.

The stone shell of the abbey was brimful with it, like a great mould waiting to be inverted and turned out in the ancient landscape. A sandcastle of shimmering invisibility, dominant amid the dark hills, twisting rivers, and tangled woodlands. Every creature that lived in or near the abbey's influence felt this in the tremble of their locked codices that smouldered throughout all their generations. From the rooks and the mice, to the men whose very hands had dug the foundations, this magnetism was the principle of pilgrimage and kept the endless stream of animals passing through its consequence, their levels of attachment as constant and as fickle as the seasons.

❦

Billy didn't leave his room for a week. Not even to bid farewell to their famous guest, who had been summoned back to the great metropolis. Maudy had retrieved Billy's breakfast tray and was making her way down to the kitchen when she met the departing Prince on the stairs again. It had inadvertently become their place of intercourse, only this time she was above and he was below. He put his cases down and smiled up at her, his teeth only mildly waffling his lip. It was obvious that he had intended to leave without speaking to her.

"My dear Miss, er . . . "

This time Maudy did not intend to help him with her name.

"Thank you for your invitation, a most interesting case. I am sure it will make a fascinating case study when I write it up."

He tilted his head in a charming coquettish manner and showed even more teeth.

Maudy did not respond. The tension was broken by the horn of a taxicab in the wet street.

"Oh! My carriage awaits. Thank you for your kind hospitality," Prince said, hoisting his cases and gliding through the corridor.

"Have you settled up, Mr. Prince?"

He slowed and again looked up at her.

"Settled up?" he said as if he had never heard the phrase before and the taste of it seemed numbing in his mouth. "But I thought I was your guest?"

"Yes, sir, it has been our pleasure to give you the hospitality of the inn, but the bar tariff is another matter."

Prince flinched and ruffled his neck in his tight, stiff shirt collar.

"Most of my libations were given by your customers and the good landlord himself. I am sure if he is consulted the tariff will be dismissed."

" 'Tis Mr. Penny who brought up the matter and asked me to remind you before you left."

Another rictus snagged up under Prince's top lip and made his right shoulder lift and fall rapidly just as the taxi's horn sounded again, louder and more impatient than before. The ruckus was in time with his nervous actions and made him look like a badly operated or tangled marionette. The juddering dance was only held in place by the anchoring weight of his suitcases.

"I see," he said.

He spat out against his teeth, which were now protruding to the fullest length so far.

"You will just have to send me the bill."

"No trouble. I have already made it out so we can settle up."

With concealed triumph she flapped the paper out of her apron pocket while holding the breakfast tray on one hand. She was down the stairs and through the bar flap before Prince had time to argue or complain.

He had to pass her to get to the street and she announced the price as he drew parallel. It was prodigious in relationship to the meagre tariff of his bed and board. He scrutinised it with great care, noting that the "drinks on the house" had been justly eliminated from the bill. The horn sounded again and he dug deep into his pocket for his cheque book and pen, signing the paper with a malice strong enough to tear the paper, which it was just about to do when the entire reservoir of black ink gushed out of the pen with an arterial force that made both parties back away in alarm. The bar counter, cheque book and bill were swimming in ink, as was the cuff of his shirt and tweed suit. The expletives he snarled at the "Ben Nevis" would even have surprised the natives of his childhood home on the Old Kent Road. Maudy simply fetched a bar towel and began wiping the black sea away, while saying firmly,

"Cash would do just as well."

Prince had wiped most of the excess off and was daintily trying to put his stained hand into his trouser pockets without further besmirching the expensive, absorbent tweed. Outside it was raining and the last of the snow had turned to limpid slush. The taxi driver gunned his engine to indicate that we he was ready for departure, passenger or not. Prince was cursing under his portcullis breath and throwing money on the ink-stained counter. When she considered there was enough, Maudy thanked the famous man and bade him a good journey home. Prince stormed out of the inn, furious and spitting venom. Maudy picked the money out of the ink and remembered the heavy ancient coins of the monk.

After she had wiped down the cash and put it in the cash register she returned with a new damp cloth to clean up the black stain. In the middle of it was the disregarded rumpled cheque with the theatrical histrionic signature. She could also just make out his printed name and the fleet of post-nominal letters behind it, initials of distinction, many of which she did not know. Acronyms that she had never heard of. She would not have been alone in that.

William Penny finally made it downstairs, but he wasn't ever the same man. He sat nervously in the corner of the bar and kept a watery eye on the doors. His abstinence evolved into the mild consumption of porter and rum, which he would explain was an almost non-alcoholic version of his previous tipple of ale and whiskey. Maudy took on all the responsibilities of the inn, working from early morn to late eve, often by herself in the anti-social hours. Especially in the first light of day, when, while everyone else was sleeping, she would take a bowl of cold leftover food and a mug of warm milk, and place it under the yellow-painted coach.

She did that every day for the next twenty-five years of her sincere and gentle life.

Acknowledgements

My thanks and respect to Brian J. Showers for inviting me to swim in the excellent Swan River. And to Timothy J. Jarvis for his skill with the text and including me with such distinguished cast on the cover note. To Dave McKean for his sumptuous, stunningly accurate vision and extension of all things that dwell within. To Meggan Kehrli, Jim Rockhill, and Ken Mackenzie for their measured patience and sharp eyes.

Special Thanks to Flossie Catling and Caroline Wirth Ullman who had the grubby job of translation at the coalface of my original manuscript.

And to my first readers whose enthusiasm and enjoyment keeps the wheel turning: Iain & Anna Sinclair, Geoff Cox, Alan Moore, Ray Cooper, Caroline again, Tony Grisoni, Sarah Simblet, Jo Welsh, Mark Booth, and my wonderful agent Millie Hoskins at United Agents. And to Dorchester-on-Thames; it's abbey, pubs, landscape, ghosts, and stories. And the memory of Rebecca being there and laughing while reading this one.

Not to mention the living and dead who haunt the English countryside and tell stories of each other continuously.

About the Author

B. Catling, RA, was born in London in 1948. He is a poet, sculptor, filmmaker, and performance artist, who is currently making egg-tempera paintings and writing novels. He has had solo exhibitions and performances in the United Kingdom, Spain, Japan, Iceland, Israel, Holland, Norway, Germany, Greenland, USA, and Australia. His *Vorrh* trilogy and novel *Earwig* have drawn much critical acclaim. He is also Emeritus Professor of Fine Art at the Ruskin School of Art, University of Oxford.

SWAN RIVER PRESS

Founded in 2003, Swan River Press is an independent publishing company, based in Dublin, Ireland, dedicated to gothic, supernatural, and fantastic literature. We specialise in limited edition hardbacks, publishing fiction from around the world with an emphasis on Ireland's contributions to the genre.

www.swanriverpress.ie

"Handsome, beautifully made volumes . . .
altogether irresistible."

– Michael Dirda, *Washington Post*

"It [is] often down to small, independent, specialist presses
to keep the candle of horror fiction flickering . . . "

– Darryl Jones, *Irish Times*

"Swan River Press has emerged as one of the most inspiring
new presses over the past decade. Not only are the books
beautifully presented and professionally produced, but they
aspire consistently to high literary quality and originality,
ranging from current writers of supernatural/weird fiction
to rare or forgotten works by departed authors."

– Peter Bell, *Ghosts & Scholars*

GREEN TEA

J. Sheridan Le Fanu

Published alongside "Carmilla" in the landmark collection *In a Glass Darkly* (1872), Le Fanu's "Green Tea" was first serialised in Charles Dickens' magazine *All the Year Round* in 1869. Since its first publication, Le Fanu's tale has lost none of its potency. "Green Tea" tells of the good natured Reverend Jennings, who writes late at night on arcane topics abetted by a steady supply of green tea. Is he insane or have these nocturnal activities opened an "interior sight" that affords a route of entry for an increasingly malignant simian companion? This 150th anniversary edition of "Green Tea", with illustrations by Alisdair Wood and an introduction by Matthew Holness, is the definitive celebration of Le Fanu's masterpiece of psychological terror and despair.

> *"Even 150 years after it was published,*
> *'Green Tea' has stood firmly against the test of time as a*
> *wonderfully eerie and well-crafted ghost story."*

> – *Ghosts & Scholars*

> *"To paraphrase Little Women, it wouldn't be Christmas*
> *without any ghost stories . . . Swan River Press*
> *has just issued a beautiful keepsake volume of*
> *J. Sheridan Le Fanu's Green Tea."*

> – Michael Dirda, *Washington Post*

OLD ALBERT

Brian J. Showers

The place is Larkhill House, and during its century and a half of existence it has hosted an array of peculiar tenants: the reclusive though brilliant ornithologist Ellis Grimwood; a murderous wine merchant and his young wife; and the Sacred Order of the Mysteries of Thoth, who re-christened Larkhill the "New Temple of Abtiti" and practised there their outlandish and mystical rites. After vacating Larkhill, these individuals—all of them—left something of themselves behind . . . Set in the same haunted neighbourhood as the stories in the award-winning collection The Bleeding Horse, Old Albert continues with the idea that not all is well in the leafy Victorian suburb of Rathmines, Dublin.

*"A strange and troubling book,
and in many ways a brilliant one."*

– Le Fanu Studies

*"Showers fills his stories with notes that mimic reality
but may or may not be based in reality."*

– The Agony Column

*"Showers works on his readers by creating an illusion of
cool objectivity, so that when he delivers his final
enigmatic denouement, it is genuinely troubling."*

– Reggie Oliver, Wormwood

THE PALE BROWN THING

Fritz Lieber

*"The ancient Egyptians only buried people
in their pyramids. We are living in ours."*

– Thibaut de Castries

Serialised in 1977, *The Pale Brown Thing* is a shorter version
of Fritz Leiber's World Fantasy Award-winning novel of
the supernatural, *Our Lady of Darkness*. Leiber maintained
that the two texts "should be regarded as the same story
told at different times"; thus this volume reprints *The Pale
Brown Thing* for the first time in nearly forty years, with
an introduction by the author's friend, Californian poet
Donald Sidney-Fryer. The novella stands as Leiber's vision
of 1970s San Francisco: a city imbued with an eccentric
vibe and nefarious entities, in which pulp writer Franz
Westen uncovers an alternate portrait of the city's *fin de
siècle* literary set—Ambrose Bierce, Jack London, Clark
Ashton Smith—as well as the darker invocations of oc-
cultist Thibaut de Castries and a pale brown inhabitant
of Corona Heights.

*"Leiber has constructed a plot in which every single detail
adds to the whole, with suggestion and implication
used to stunning effect, so that our sense of dread mounts."*

– *Black Static*

www.ingramcontent.com/pod-product-compliance
Ingram Content Group UK Ltd.
Pitfield, Milton Keynes, MK11 3LW, UK
UKHW041411020125
3930UKWH00037B/318

9 781783 807451